Ben's head was inches from hers.

His startling eyes watched her with an intensity that reached deep inside her, and the mouth that could do the most amazing things on her skin looked soft after sleep. His arm was still on her waist, only now she was being pulled closer to his body.

'I've missed you, Tori. I've missed *us*.'

'We were great together.' What was she talking about? Their lovemaking? Or everything? Their life, their love—everything.

'Did we give up too easily?' he whispered, just before his lips brushed her forehead, then trailed down her cheek to her mouth.

'Ben…' she cried softly against his mouth, and her lips opened, pressed against his. Ben. Benji. Her heart.

Their mouths became one, moulded together.

I remember this.

Ben pulled her closer still, so there was only the bedcover between them. All the while they kissed. Her eyes were wide open, watching him, drinking in every line, each eyebrow hair, the eyes that were watching her back. Benji.

This was us.

Kissing Benji had always been her favourite way to start the day. His passion and love had set her up and made her feel good.

As she was beginning to feel now.

Dear Reader,

Since I was tiny I've dreamed of going to France, after seeing photos of my dad in Paris. I learned French at school, and never stopped dreaming of making it there. But life kept me busy with other things and it wasn't until 2013 that I got there. What a wonderful trip! I couldn't get enough of Paris or Nice—the locations I've used in this story. And what really topped off my dream trip was finding my books on the shelves in bookshops in Gare du Nord in Paris and the main railway station in Tours.

Ben and Tori once shared a love that never really finished. Life interrupted and gave them too many problems to cope with, breaking their marriage. Now, in France for a cardiology conference, they're both getting their second chance. But with Tori working in Auckland and Ben in London it's not going to be easy for them, so they have to make the most of the few days they have together.

I hope you enjoy their journey as they thrash out the problems that divided them seven years earlier. I'd love to hear what you think. Email me at sue.mackay56@yahoo.com, or drop by at suemackay.co.nz

Cheers!

Sue

REUNITED...IN PARIS!

BY
SUE MacKAY

First published in Great Britain 2015
by Mills & Boon, an imprint of Harlequin (UK) Limited,
Eton House, 18-24 Paradise Road, Richmond, Surrey, TW9 1SR

© 2015 Sue MacKay

ISBN: 978-0-263-25884-4

Harlequin (UK) Limited's policy is to use papers that are natural, renewable and recyclable products and made from wood grown in sustainable forests. The logging and manufacturing processes conform to the legal environmental regulations of the country of origin.

Printed and bound in Great Britain
by CPI Antony Rowe, Chippenham, Wiltshire

With a background of working in medical laboratories, and a love of the romance genre, it is no surprise that **Sue MacKay** writes Mills & Boon® Medical Romance™ stories. An avid reader all her life, she wrote her first story at age eight—about a prince, of course. She lives with her own hero in the beautiful Marlborough Sounds, at the top of New Zealand's South Island, where she indulges her passions for the outdoors, the sea and cycling.

Books by Sue MacKay

Mills & Boon® Medical Romance™

Doctors to Daddies
A Father for Her Baby
The Midwife's Son

The Family She Needs
A Family This Christmas
From Duty to Daddy
The Gift of a Child
You, Me and a Family
Christmas with Dr Delicious
Every Boy's Dream Dad
The Dangers of Dating Your Boss
Surgeon in a Wedding Dress
Midwife...to Mum!

**Visit the author profile page
at millsandboon.co.uk for more titles**

This book is dedicated to three very special people—
my man, Lindsay, and our closest friends,
Jill and Kevin Turner, who joined us in Paris
to celebrate my big birthday in 2013. Thanks to all of
you for making the occasion something to be treasured.

Praise for Sue MacKay

'A deeply emotional, heart-rending story that will make you smile and make you cry. I truly recommend it—and don't miss the second book: the story about Max.'

—*HarlequinJunkie* on
The Gift of a Child

'What a great book. I loved it. I did not want it to end. This is one book not to miss.'

—*GoodReads* on
The Gift of a Child

CHAPTER ONE

TORI WELLS STOOD just inside the entrance to the massive conference room in Hôtel de Nice and swallowed hard, digging deep for composure as she scanned the sea of faces and listened to the many languages swirling back and forth. It wouldn't do her reputation any good to go around grinning like a clown.

The excitement that had been gripping her since her plane had taken off from Auckland International two days ago threatened to spill over and have her dancing on the spot in her new and very gorgeous avocado-green high heels. French, of course. As for the price tag, she could've fed a very small nation but for once didn't feel guilty at all about indulging her passion. Not even the littlest bit.

Accepting the invitation to speak in front of all these people had been a no-brainer. Even though she doubted that world-famous experts would be interested in what a cardiologist from New Zealand had to say about heart problems in children who'd suffered from rheumatic fever, she hadn't been able to say no to the director of the Cardiac Forum. She'd have come if Monsieur Leclare had asked her to talk about racing snails in the sand, the opportunity to visit France being too awesome to miss. He could've saved many euros if only he'd known she'd have slept in a tent on the beach if necessary, but he'd promised, and delivered, a suite in a beautiful hotel overlooking the stunning Mediterranean Sea. The Mediterranean Sea. Her excitement intensified, gripping her.

And then... She grinned. And then he wanted her to go to Paris after this convention to talk to medical students about her work. Oh—my—goodness. Paris. How cool was that? Her hands squeezed tight and she squashed her lips together to hold back the joy from spilling out loud.

'Hello, Tori. I've been looking out for you.'

The excitement vanished in a flash. Gone. The air chilled. She shivered. *Benji? Here?* She'd checked. His name hadn't been on the programme. But that was definitely his voice. *Turn around and acknowledge him. Can't.* Her lungs had stopped working. Her composure had gone to hell in a barrow. *Do it. Face him.*

Slowly gathering a steadying breath, she turned to lock gazes with her ex-husband. 'Hello, Ben.'

Her tongue felt huge in her dry mouth. He looked... stunning. As usual. But different. Older, of course. World-weary, like he'd taken a hit somewhere over the years. Hardly surprising given the circumstances surrounding them seven years ago when he'd walked out on her. Finally she managed, 'What are you doing here?'

Lady Luck had thrown a wild card. No, make that a grenade. Fragments of pain, anger, bewilderment, even need, cut into her, making a mockery of what had become her well-put-back-together life.

'I'm a last-minute fill-in for one of the partners I work for. He's handling a family crisis back in London.'

The voice she'd have to be dead not to recognise whispered across her skin, reminding her body of things she didn't want to recall. Hot nights on the beach in Fiji, where they'd gone for their honeymoon. The first time he'd taken her on a date—at the hospital cafeteria because they'd had less than an hour between shifts in the cardiology surgical department. *I don't want to remember those times.* She used to call him Benji. Too intimate. Too loaded with memories.

Tori reached for normality, came up with, 'How are you finding living in London?'

His smile appeared genuine, but appearances could be deceptive, had become so with Ben in those last bewildering months before he'd left. To be fair, which she mostly was, she had no idea what he was like these days. And didn't want to know. *Oh, really?*

Ben replied, 'I'm working towards a partnership in the cardiology clinic I've joined, so I don't have a lot of free time, but when I do I indulge my passion for English history by visiting more castles and historic homes than even I could've imagined back in NZ.' He wasn't having trouble talking, made it seem perfectly normal to be chatting with her for the first time since he'd said goodbye on the doorstep of their apartment. Tears had been streaming down his cheeks then. Tears he'd tried hard to hide from her.

Concentrate on what Ben had just said, act like this was nothing to be in such a turmoil over. He'd mentioned castles. She used to buy him books filled with photos of the most stunning homes set in the English countryside. 'The château at Mount Ruapehu doesn't quite compare, then?' Thinking of the tourist hotel back home where they'd stayed for their first wedding anniversary made her smile tightly despite the way her heart was pitter-pattering in her chest.

Stop smiling. He'll think you're happy to see him.

'No comparison at all.' Ben was no longer smiling.

She could see in his eyes the memory of those wonderful couple of days spent in the snow and back in their hotel room afterwards. She also saw regret. For stopping to talk to her? Why *had* she mentioned the château? It was loaded with their history.

Then Ben straightened even taller and stole her breath with, 'You're looking fabulous.' The words were glib and exactly what she'd expect. He'd always been an expert in saying the right thing. Not always the whole truth and nothing but the truth at the end, but definitely always the right thing.

These days she'd learned to do glib, too, and so could ignore the compliment. 'Why, Ben, thank you.' If she said 'Ben' often enough then surely her brain would get the idea and forget *Benji* had ever existed.

'I mean it,' he said softly, sincerely.

Talk about knocking her in the back of her knees. Any second now her legs were going to dump her in a heap in the midst of this crowd. At Ben's feet. 'Thank you,' she squeaked.

She was stunned. It had been seven years since she'd seen Benji—*Ben*, damn it—and the circumstances back then had been too awful to ever want to revisit. Long, lonely years in which she'd struggled to get over him, to put their failed marriage behind her and make life work in a way she could be proud of. She'd thought she'd succeeded, right up until this moment when her heart was beating like a drum. Like they had unfinished business, or something equally ridiculous. Crazy, because she'd loved him with her whole being, and then he'd gone and left her and she'd had to face life without him at her side. Then there'd been the tragedy that had occurred weeks later that she'd had to deal with on her own.

A few minutes in his company and her brain was

stalling, unable to bring up anything coherent and sensible to say. She was well-known for her good sense back home at her clinic. But this was a rerun of those months towards the end when she hadn't known how to talk to Ben without feeling like she'd been underwater, slowly drowning.

A woman jostled her as she squeezed past and Ben stepped closer, using his body to shield her from the stream of people now pouring into the enormous room. He touched his hand to her elbow. Contrition darkened those eyes that she'd always called pools of caramel. 'Tori, I've upset you by appearing out of nowhere. I'm sorry.'

Hello? This definitely wasn't Benji. An apology? To her? He'd said more words in the last couple of minutes than he had in the final months of their marriage. She studied him quickly, thoroughly. The intervening years had added a depth to his gaze, deeper lines at the corners of his mouth, and a few grey hairs in his dark curls, but it was definitely the Benji she'd once loved with all her heart. A long time ago. Except the man of her past hadn't done apologies. No, he'd packed his bags, said bye, and gone out the front door, out of her life. So this had to be Ben, not Benji. See, she was getting better at this already. Ben.

Tori gave a nonchalant shrug that hopefully hid the storm of emotions battering at her, and at the same time removed his hand. She didn't need reminding of the heat that used to consume them at every touch. Lovemaking had never been an issue between them. 'I'm not upset. Just surprised to see you. That's all.' If she said it often enough she might start believing herself. Glancing around, she was amazed at how quickly the chairs were filling. 'I need to find a seat.'

'Come on.' Those fingers were back at her elbow, turning her toward the front. 'Monsieur Leclare sent me to escort you to where you're sitting with the other speakers.'

'But I'm not on until tomorrow.'

Ben led her along the side of the auditorium, again protecting her from the crowd. 'All the speakers are requested to sit in the front row for the duration of the conference.'

She hadn't got that memo. So there'd be no getting away from Ben while she absorbed the shock of seeing him. Seeing him and hearing again that deep, gravelly voice she'd fallen in love with the first time he'd spoken to her would take some getting used to. Right now she didn't have time to think about her reaction to him. *You're not angry with him any more.* After all those years she shouldn't be. That'd suggest she was still keeping him alive in her heart. And she definitely wasn't doing that. Ben was history, no more, no less.

'Madame Wells—the Heart Lady.' Monsieur Leclare stood in front of her, greeting her with the traditional kisses to both cheeks. So typically European that her excitement began returning. 'I'm thrilled to meet you in person, and thank you for coming so far to talk to us.'

Tori listened carefully to his heavily accented English, and found him a smile. A Frenchman speaking her language was intriguing, and a little bit romantic—even if this cardiologist was in his sixties and looking decidedly the worse for wear. She'd done basic French at school in Auckland but the few times she'd tried to make herself understood since arriving in Nice yesterday hadn't been very successful, her accent apparently a disaster. '*Monsieur le docteur*, I'm honoured and thrilled to be here.'

'Please, I'm Luc. Is this is your first visit to France?'

'Yes. Coming here has been on my bucket list since I was a teenager.'

'Bucket list?' he asked. 'What is this?'

'It's a list of things I want to achieve in my lifetime. People make them all the time. Visiting Paris will be ticked off by the time I return home.'

Ben wasn't to be left out. 'I imagine Tori's got going to see the Moulin Rouge somewhere on that list. She loves shows.'

'Ah...*la liste de choses à faire*. Now I understand.' Luc smiled. 'It is good you are going to Paris. It is the city of romance.' He gave Ben a knowing nod. 'My assistant will arrange a table at the show for you.'

Tori quickly shook her head. 'Thank you, but I've got other arrangements in place.' *And I'd only need one ticket.*

Luc was smiling happily and ignoring her reply. 'No, you must go. It will be my pleasure.'

Tori managed a thank-you. Going to the city of love on her own was pathetic enough, but going to Moulin Rouge alone, with a spare ticket? Downright tragic.

Ben replied, 'Thank you. We look forward to it.'

Disappointment and envy unfurled inside Tori. Of course there'd be a woman in his life. The man didn't do solo. Was she here at the hotel? Out spending bags of money while Ben was at the conference?

Does it matter? You're over him.

'Madame Wells, Monsieur Wells, please be seated. I will talk to you some more tonight at the dinner.'

Ben nodded before turning back to Tori. 'Why haven't you changed your surname back to Carter?'

She didn't want to talk about that. Not here. Not ever. She went for flip. 'Think of the expense and all the mess-ing around involved in changing practising licences, passport, the property title for the apartment. Far easier to leave things as they are.'

'I'd have thought it would be the first thing you did on becoming single again.' He looked bewildered, and a little pleased. 'You're still living in our apartment?'

Forget it, Benji. It's my apartment nowadays. If she was being honest she hadn't moved out or changed her name because—well, because that meant the final cut from him, and at the time of their divorce she hadn't been ready for that. 'If it's bugging you I'll get on to sorting it the moment I get home.' But she wouldn't move out of the apartment that she'd always adored and where she'd created a little sanctuary for herself by re-painting in different colours and changing the furniture to remove memories.

Tori dropped onto the first vacant chair in the front row. Ben was here. In Nice. At the conference. Her stomach knotted.

He stood beside her. 'Do you mind if I join you?'

'Do I have a choice?' she snapped, then instantly regretted her tone. But she wanted to be alone. Okay, it was hard to be alone in the midst of hundreds of people, but if only Ben would go and sit somewhere else to give her time to get over their first meeting.

He looked along the row, shook his head. 'No, I'm afraid not.' Then he smiled. 'I promise I won't cause you any trouble.'

Translated, that meant he'd be charming and cordial so as to win her over, because he'd be hating it that she hadn't fallen all over him. Charm was his modus operandi. It won him anything, anyone he aspired to. Well, it wouldn't work with her. Not any more. 'Fine.' She crossed her legs and turned to face the stage directly in front.

Except he'd already caused her trouble just by being here. Her tumbling emotions had her in a pickle. Benji had been her first love, her only love. Did that mean this was a normal reaction, and that once she'd got over the shock of seeing him she'd be able to hold a conversation with him without wanting to touch his arms, his chest, face? The air huffed over her bottom lip. Touch Ben? That would go down like a ton of bricks. He'd back off fast—which might be the answer to the situation.

No, she'd try ignoring him, focus entirely on the speakers. Unfortunately it was too soon to put on the headphones supplied so attendees could hear translations in their own language when the talks started. Those would blank out Benji, but she'd have to wait. Sitting up straight, Tori breathed deeply. And smelt a scrummy combination of citrus and pine. 'You still use the same aftershave.'

He leaned close. 'It's my favourite.'

Oh, blast. Had she really said that out loud? Now he'd definitely have the wrong idea. She tried shallow breathing to avoid smelling that scent. It didn't work. Instead the air suddenly seemed full of the evocative, promise-laden smell, almost as though she was in a lemon grove surrounded by pine trees—with Benji. It overwhelmed her and brought back another memory. The aftershave had been an impulse buy after their first date. She'd wrapped it in white paper with red hearts printed on it. On their second date, when he'd taken her to bed for the first time, he'd stripped down to his undies—white ones with red hearts splashed across them.

I've got to get out of here. I'll stand at the back of the room. She began to push up on her feet. Loud applause broke out and Tori sank back down. Too late. She wasn't moving anywhere. The conference had begun. Putting her hands together, she joined in.

Monsieur Leclare stood in front of the microphone. '*Mesdames et messieurs*, welcome to the tenth European Cardiac Forum. We are lucky to have some wonderful speakers whom I'm sure you'll be thrilled to listen to over the next three days.'

Settling farther back on her chair, Tori pinched herself. *I'm in France. At a conference of peers from all over Europe and America.* Another pinch. *Sitting beside my ex-husband.* Her teeth clamped together. She suddenly felt ill.

Then Benji moved, and his elbow touched her arm. She hated the warmth filtering through her, ramping up the tension that had been gripping her since she'd first heard him say hello.

'Stand up,' he whispered warmly. 'They're applauding you.'

Leaping up, Tori turned to face the auditorium, blinked like a rabbit in headlights and dredged up a smile. *What are they all doing, clapping me?* She nodded left and right. *Now I'm behaving like royalty. Should've stayed back in Kiwi land where I'm just an ordinary girl.*

'Now I'd like to introduce the members of the panel for Friday. Benjamin Wells, cardiac surgeon from London.' Luc Leclare introduced the other three specialists Ben would be talking with about a new technique they'd developed for post heart-transplant recovery.

As the men stood the applause increased tenfold. Tori sank back onto her chair, automatically clapping along with everyone else, feeling something very like pride for Ben leaking into her psyche. He was clever, had always been totally focused on cardiology and his patients.

While he was distracted by the applause she took

the opportunity to study him once more. *Can't you get enough of him?* Her lungs faltered. He'd been handsome, but add seven years and the drama of dealing with the unnecessary and controversial death of his patient, their break-up and those youthful good looks had toughened, tightened, making him even more good-looking. He suited who he'd become.

Ben finally sat down, and leaned close. 'You're staring.'

'Just making sure I know who I'm sharing the front row with.'

'And do you? Know me?' A sad glint appeared in his eyes and his mouth flattened.

'Do you still talk in funny voices and sing off-key while shaving?'

He shook his head. 'Don't have the time any more.'

He used to make time. 'Sleep on your stomach?'

'No.'

Another change. 'Want six kids?'

'I'd settle for one.'

He'd nearly got one. Her stomach hit the floor. The baby. Their baby, the one she'd lost and that he knew nothing about.

'How am I doing?' Ben asked.

Somehow she managed to croak out, 'No, I don't know you.' She tried to find him a smile but was all out of them. Instead she muttered, 'If you don't mind, I would like to listen to the director.'

She had to look away from those eyes that saw too much, knew too much and had always got him what he wanted. Shame he hadn't felt the same about her. They might've resolved some of their problems before they'd got out of hand. Not getting caught up in the web of fun and charm that was Benjamin Wells over the next few days would be the toughest challenge since their break-up. He came with too many memories, good and bad, for them to be able to step around the minefield and get along as though the past hadn't happened.

Ben didn't blame Tori for the cold shoulder she was working so hard to give him. If, back in London, he'd had more than twelve hours' notice and hadn't been frantically handing over patients to his colleagues he'd have tried to let her know that he'd be here, just to save any embarrassment. Except neither of them had been embarrassed—more shaken than anything.

How could he have forgotten how beautiful Tori was? He'd fallen in love with those classic features, perfect skin and twinkling emerald eyes. Fallen in a flash. One look across a frantically busy department had been all it had taken. Then he'd spoken to her and she'd laughed and that had been the ribbon on the box that was his heart. If he closed his eyes he could bring up the images of that morning right now. It had been her first day at Auckland's specialist cardiac hospital, and she'd been sent to the department where he'd worked as a surgeon, trying to get up the hours and experience to go into private practice.

I've missed you, Tori.

His heart stalled. Got away, he had not. He'd refused to.

Yes, I have missed you. I'm only just beginning to admit it, but I have. I haven't looked seriously at another woman since you. Haven't wanted to.

As he watched Tori chatting to two conference attendees he felt a deep hunger opening up inside.

For Tori.

But they were finished. As in never-to-repeat-that-experience-again finished. Tori wouldn't let him within a bull's roar of her except in a crowded space like this. He'd hurt her beyond belief—for all the right reasons, or so he'd believed at the time. But later, when the flak died away and he'd had more than enough hours to reflect, he'd accepted he'd been lashing out at her for not believing in him, for not trusting him to be the consummate professional when operating on a patient—because she'd been right. His shame had been consuming him even before she'd questioned his integrity. Afterwards it had known no boundaries. If his wife couldn't believe in him, who could? Not even his father had questioned his guilt, instead focusing on trying to hide it by laying the blame elsewhere, which had made the situation far worse.

Seeing Tori after all this time, touching her elbow, breathing the same air, had stirred up this intense hunger within him. *Seriously?* It couldn't be hunger for Tori. They had far too many unresolved issues that they hadn't been able to fix back when they'd been married. Even if he explained why he'd called it quits on their marriage there wasn't a chance in Hades of Tori ever trusting him completely and thereby loving him again.

Even at the worst moments of their failing marriage he'd wished her the absolute best in her career, her private life, in everything she desired. Always. Then after their divorce he'd wanted it even more. He'd owed her for pushing her away at a time he'd desperately needed her. She'd known his need and he could still see the hurt in her eyes every time he'd denied her. He owed her for so many things, and at the same time he'd been slayed by her accusation. But he hadn't been able to bring himself to admit the truth to her.

'Ben, there you are. I've been searching this crowd

from the moment we were released for coffee. How the blazes are you? It's been a while.'

Ben turned to find John standing beside him and clasped his hand. 'Released? You make it sound like a sentence being here. How're things with you? It's been a long time.' Hell, John had gained a lot of weight since they'd last caught up.

'Too long, but I guess it's too far for you to hop a ride down to Sydney to play catch-up.' John sounded like he wished for exactly that.

'It's not next door, that's for sure.' But it was his turn to visit and he should've made the effort. John had been a good friend to him while he'd lived in Sydney, trying to get back on his feet. 'I'll head your way next time I pull holidays. How's that?' Talk about an instant decision. There'd be no backing out once John's wife, Rita, heard.

'Deal.' John's gaze drifted sideways to where Tori stood. 'So that's your ex-wife.'

'Tori.' John would've heard her name when she'd been introduced at the conference. Because they shared the same surname, would everyone here think he and Tori were married? He didn't know what to make of that. Her explanation for not changing back to her maiden name didn't ring true of her. Not the Tori he'd known, who'd always done what had needed doing without delay. Whenever he'd read 'Tori Wells' in an article or, recently, on the forum programme, he'd know a moment of pleasure—before reality had set in. They were divorced. Sharing a name meant nothing, held no connection.

John was still yabbering in his ear. 'Got a surprise when "Madame Wells" stood up. I knew she was coming, but you never said she was a looker.'

A change of subject was needed urgently. 'Is Rita here, too?'

'You don't think I'd be allowed to come to France without her, do you?' John grinned. 'I hate to think what's happening to the credit card right now.'

'Go, Rita. I hope she blows the budget big time.' Ben knew the diminutive woman who was the light of his friend's life would be very circumspect. She came from a poor background and having money on tap hadn't made her a spendthrift, though being in France might tempt her to have some fun. He'd always liked Rita, and had felt envious of the relationship she and John shared. The kind of relationship he and Tori had had in the beginning—before his monumental error of judgement. Stop thinking about Tori. It wouldn't get him anywhere. Focus on John. 'How's life at Sydney Hospital?'

'Muddling along. Never enough time to see all the patients I'd like to, but otherwise no complaints. What about you? You're still happy on Harley Street?'

'Absolutely. It takes up most of my time.' And filled in the end of the day when everyone else was at home with family while he only had a solitary meal prepared by his housekeeper to look forward to. 'It's turned into a twenty-four-seven career.'

Except for the next few days. Hopefully he'd get to relax a bit. He was exhausted and needed a break before he made a mistake. *Another mistake.* A shudder rolled through him. He had learned the hard way to routinely take leave to recharge his batteries. An overtired surgeon made mistakes. Shifting his balance from one foot to the other, he noticed John grinning at him. 'Did I miss something?'

'I don't believe it. You're working all hours. No play time? What about the ladies? Surely you're keeping up with them?'

Ben's eyes were drawn to that perfectly coiffed red

hair a few metres away. Now, there was a lady, a real lady. One whose agenda had never been to want to hang off his arm because he'd been endowed with good looks, or to make use of his wealth, or to be 'seen' with Mr Benjamin Wells, surgeon. No, she'd loved him for himself, including all his faults. Or so he'd thought until those last months. Seemed he might've got that wrong, given she was obviously over him.

He turned back to John. 'I haven't joined the monastery, if that's what you're inferring.' But he kept every encounter light and friendly. No one ever had to teach him the same lesson twice.

'You ever think of heading back down our way permanently? Or are you firmly ensconced in England?'

Ben contemplated the question. He'd enjoyed his time in Sydney where the culture was so similar to home that he'd fitted in easily. London was different. He loved the city with its shows and nightlife, the history and art. His apartment overlooking the Thames was a dream come true. But he never felt he belonged. 'When the rain doesn't stop bucketing down for days on end, or there's a polar blast happening, then, yes, I give the idea a glance. But, no, I'm a Londoner now.' Or so he tried to convince himself. Especially on the days when homesickness for Auckland turned him sour.

Before he could stop himself, his gaze cruised over Tori again, and his mouth dried as he glimpsed her creamy throat as she tipped her head back to laugh. He couldn't see it under that ivory blouse and green jacket but there was a small mole centimetres below her right clavicle. Anyone watching her wouldn't know how wild that abundant red hair was when let loose from the restraints she currently had it held in, how it spilled across the pillow and felt like satin in his hands.

'Time we returned to our seats,' John said. 'Want to meet Rita and me in the bar before the dinner tonight?'

'Six-thirty suit?' A couple of drinks and some relaxed conversation with good friends were just the ticket to put Tori out of his head for a while.

Not that he expected to be totally free of her for the duration of the conference, but right now any time without her within sight, disturbing his carefully put-together equilibrium, had to be good. Didn't it?

CHAPTER TWO

IN ANOTHER NEW pair of gorgeous shoes, red this time, Tori followed the waiter to her table for the formal dinner. Across the crowd already seated she saw Benji standing in the distance, a distance that inexorably became smaller and smaller until she was led right up to him. 'There has to be some mistake.'

But there on the table, in black on a gilt-edged card, was written 'Madame Wells' in calligraphy, marking her place. Right next to the card naming the one person out of more than twelve hundred she did not want to sit with.

Apparently totally unperturbed, Ben gave his gut-twisting smile as he pulled out her chair. 'Would've been more interesting if the same mistake had been made over our hotel rooms.'

'In your dreams, Benji.' Gulp. 'Ben.' Too late.

That smile went virile, wide and open and full of laughter. Then he leaned closer to whisper, 'I can't believe you just said Benji.' Then his smile dipped and that sadness she'd witnessed in the morning was back, his cheeky streak taking a hike.

She turned her back on him. What else could she do? He'd totally unnerved her with that flip comment about their rooms, and yet it shouldn't have. Being stuck at the same table didn't mean she had to spend all night con-

centrating on Ben—even when a part of her wanted to
do exactly that. Glancing around the table to see if she
knew anyone else, she found a woman of similar age to
her watching the whole incident with amusement. Tori
felt her blood begin to boil. Why did strangers enjoy
other people's discomfort? The dinner hadn't begun and
already she wanted to leave.

Then the woman stuck her hand across the table. 'Hi,
I'm Rita McIntyre. That's my husband, John, next to
Ben.'

Tori drew on her reserves to push away her negativ-
ity and took the hand being offered. It was as warm as
the friendly expression on Rita's face. 'I'm Tori Wells.'

Rita nodded. 'I thought so. It's really good to meet
you. We've known Ben since he moved to Sydney from
New Zealand. He and John worked together at Sydney
Hospital and we all became firm friends, though we
haven't seen enough of him since he shifted to London.
We're trying to entice him back Down Under so we're
able to catch up more often. Our kids miss him a lot.'

Too much information. Instantly a picture of Ben
kicking a ball around a yard with children filled her
head. Ben cuddling an unhappy child. Ben buying the
biggest ice creams available for kids. He'd have been a
wonderful dad, given the chance. Tori gulped, nodded
and looked around for a waiter. A glass of water wouldn't
go amiss. *I don't need to know any of this. It's his life,
nothing to do with me. But I wanted that with him, too.
Nearly had it, in fact.*

Ben grumped at Rita, 'I'm not sure Tori wants to
talk about me.'

Rita was made of sterner stuff. 'Of course she does.
Bet she's kept an eye on your career, as you have hers.
Isn't that right, Tori?'

Eek. Ben's kept up to date with what I've been doing? Now what? Tell the truth. It can't hurt. 'You're right. I have.' By the surprise on Ben's face she should've kept quiet. 'He's done extremely well, but that was probably a given from the day he started med school.' *Whoa, Tori, haul on the brakes, will you?*

She glanced around. Where was a waiter when she needed one? So Ben had also followed her career, which explained how he'd known she hadn't changed her name. Seems neither of them had let go of the other entirely. Suddenly she felt warm inside. It was kind of interesting that Ben did want to know what she'd been up to, hadn't written her off completely.

Glancing up at her ex standing beside her, Tori felt that warmth spread farther out into the corners of her body.

'Thank you for your compliment. I've been lucky to have done well recently,' he said.

They both knew about the luck, or lack of it. There was no conceit in his voice any more, just a quiet belief in himself. A steadier version of the man she'd married, that belief tempered with reality. But, then, he'd learned the hard way to be humble as far as his career went.

Rita grinned like she'd won a prize at the carnival. 'Ben, sit down, for goodness' sake. Snap those fingers and get us some drinks ordered. Tori and I have some serious talking to do.' She turned her formidable gaze onto Tori. 'Where did you get that dress? It's amazing. I want one just like it. Maybe make that almost like it. Can't be wearing the same, can we?'

Because of Rita's forthrightness, Tori felt herself relaxing. She had nothing to hide from this woman. Except the same old story she hid from everyone. She shivered. Especially from Ben. 'I went shopping yesterday straight after I arrived and had a shower to wash off the travel skin.'

'Travel skin? I like that. I know what you mean. Spending all that time confined in a plane does make you feel less than clean, doesn't it? You weren't jet-lagged?'

'Absolutely, but I'd arrived in France. I wasn't spending the first hours sleeping. They have the most wonderful shops here. The shoes are amazing. How could I ignore those?' She felt Ben take his seat, his thigh bumping against hers before he quickly shifted away, putting a small gap between them. Her teeth slammed shut. Even the slightest touch, unintentional as it had been, shot her temperature over the moon.

'So tell me, where are these shops?' Rita asked. 'Or do you have time in your schedule to come with me?'

'I hope so. I have a few gaps in my schedule. Let me look at the programme after dinner and get back to you on that. There's a jacket I couldn't make my mind up about. I'd value your opinion.' Shopping was always a great way to spend an hour or three, and she'd also like to get to know Rita some more. Hopefully Ben wouldn't see a problem with that, considering that Rita and her husband were his friends.

Then pine scent caught at her as Ben leaned forward. 'What do you want to drink?'

Looking around, she saw a waiter hovering. 'Sparkling water, please.' Ben looked so cute when his eyebrows rose like that, sort of how she'd imagined he might've looked as a boy. Of course, he might be surprised she had given up drinking. He didn't know that she'd believed her drinking had caused the miscarriage so she hadn't touched a drop since that awful night. He hadn't known she was pregnant at all.

Anyway, she'd only started drinking heavily in the

first place when their marriage had been going pear-shaped and the alcohol had seemed to help her forget for a while, and had had the added benefit of sending her to sleep every night when thoughts of Ben and their failing love had otherwise kept her tossing and turning until the alarm had gone off in the morning. They'd been leading such separate lives by then that Ben probably hadn't even noticed how reliant she'd become on alcohol to numb her sadness.

Everyone else ordered wine, and then introductions were made between the other guests seated around the table and as the conversation became general Tori began to enjoy herself.

Until, 'Forget fabulous. You look beautiful tonight,' Ben said quietly in an interlude between the main course and a speech from the leading French cardiologist. 'Rita's right. That dress is superb on you. Black always did suit your colouring.'

But it wasn't the colour he was staring at. His gaze was locked on her cleavage.

'Drop it, Ben,' she muttered. If she'd known she was going to be seated beside him she'd have worn a sack. *Yes, and he used to say you could make sacks look like fashion statements.* Her nails dug into her palms. There were far too many memories unlocking in her brain. They'd obviously been hovering, waiting for this day to spring up and remind her of things that weren't going to do her any good remembering.

When he finally raised his head there was only sorrow in his eyes. He used to be so smug, to the point of arrogant, because he'd always got what he'd wanted. But this Ben appeared different, softer and more careful of others' feelings. She'd loved him to bits, and had been so proud of him when he'd refused to take the easy option his father had presented to save him from a blot on his CV. Doing that had to have taken guts, and obviously he'd done a lot of soul searching on the way. He'd grown, changed and yet was still her Benji. *Benji? Who's Benji? This man is Ben.*

Why did her eyes keep slipping sideways to stare at the only man she'd ever loved? The man she'd once believed she'd be spending the rest of her life with. Benji. Or Ben. Whichever. The package was the same. Sexy albeit with a healthy dose of intellect in those mouth-watering eyes.

I remember every detail of that body. How you liked being caressed just above your hip. How your muscles tightened when I licked a trail down your stomach. Oh, hell. Stop this. I'm at a dinner surrounded by hundreds of other people. With my ex-husband whom I got over years ago. It's obviously time I found a man and had a good time between the sheets.

Except that didn't cut it with her. She couldn't raise any enthusiasm. Swinging back to face across the table, she reached for her empty glass. Where was the waiter? If ever there was a time she wished she drank alcohol, now was it.

Desperate for fresh air and a little solitude, the moment the formal dinner had finally drawn to a close Tori hurried to her room to change into trousers and a blouse, and slipped on flat shoes. Her toes needed a rest from those amazing shoes.

Back in the lobby she saw Ben talking with a group of specialists from New York, but the moment he spied her walking towards the front entrance he excused himself and joined her.

'Going for a stroll along Quai des États-Unis?' he asked.

Despite wanting to remain aloof, she chuckled at his butchering of the French words. 'Yes, the fresh air is appealing, and anyway it's Nice. Why sit in my room and miss all that?' She waved a hand in the direction of the road and the Mediterranean beyond. 'I've waited most of my life to come to France, I'm not going to waste precious time hiding away.'

'What would you have to hide from, Tori?' Ben took her elbow and ushered her through the door being held open by the concierge.

You. Us. The memories you've brought with you. Easing her elbow free the moment she stood on the pavement, Tori drew warm air into her lungs, thinking fast for an answer. She didn't want to offend him, or be rude. Neither did she want to expose her vulnerability. Not when she had only just realised it was there, undermining her determination to be friendly but uninvolved with him.

'Please, don't say it's me. I don't want to spoil your time here.' Again that sincerity threatened to undermine all her intentions to keep him at arm's length.

Finally she went with, 'I find conferences tend to take all my attention so that I'm unaware of anything else around me.' It was true, but not why she wanted to keep to herself here. 'I could be in a hotel anywhere. But not this time. I'm going to make the most of every free second I have.'

Tori began walking along the promenade and Ben stepped out beside her. When had she said she'd like company? His in particular? But the words weren't there to tell him to leave her to walk alone.

'I know what you mean. These things are often held

in exotic settings and yet, like you say, the participants don't get to appreciate their surroundings.' He was speaking in that low, gravelly voice that heated her right down to her toes every time. Did he know that? Had she ever told him? She must have. 'But I'm glad you haven't stayed upstairs. It's not like you. Going for a walk at nearly midnight is the Tori I remember.'

Not for a long time. 'I'm exhausted but I don't plan on sleeping much at all until I get on that plane to go home again.'

'This is too good to miss, I agree.' Ben slipped his jacket off and hooked it over his shoulder on his forefinger. His tie had disappeared and the crisp white shirt—they'd always been his favourite attire with jackets—was unbuttoned at the top. His free hand was pushed into the pocket of his black dress trousers.

Benji at his sexiest. And most dangerous. Looking like every woman's dream come to life, he was impossible to ignore. Impossible. But she had to ignore him. He might have a hot bod, be more tempting than a sugar fix, but she could not put herself out there to be hurt.

Automatically caressing the thin gold band she wore permanently on her wrist with her finger, she let other painful memories slip into her mind, bringing tears with them. A tiny baby, nine weeks in her womb, gone in a rush of blood and anguish, to be missed for ever. The final nail in what had become a dreadful year, and Ben had never learned about their baby, hadn't known of their child's existence.

'Tori? You still with me?' Ben asked, with a hint of laughter in his voice. 'Or are you star-gazing, like you always did?'

No, I'm hurting here. Not a day had gone by that she didn't feel guilty about losing their baby. But he did not

need to know that. There was nothing Ben could do
to change the past, so why put him through the pain?
She'd plaster on a smile and go with happy and, who
knew, she might make excited before she got to the end
of the promenade. 'I'm taking it all in, absorbing the
atmosphere.'

Many tourists were making the most of the balmy,
early summer evening, laughing and talking in different languages, which made her smile with delight. She
and Ben nodded to an occasional person they recognised
from the conference, but kept away from being drawn
into conversation.

Eventually some excitement softened her taut muscles. *Nice.* Wow. It was so...foreign. Even the air smelt
different—full of history and wealth and promise.

'Is France living up to your expectations so far?'

Again that voice skidded over her skin and set her
heart tapping a different beat, adding to the strange mix
of emotions she was feeling tonight. Tori struggled to
banish that and find that happy mood she'd promised
herself, finally found a modicum of control—enough to
fool Ben, she hoped. 'Oh, yes. Absolutely.'

A quick glance sideways at him and she nearly
tripped over her own feet. She hurriedly righted herself before Ben could make a move to catch her. She
did not want to feel his fingers on her skin. No, she did
not. They'd send heat waves throughout her sex-starved
body. But he was hard to ignore. His beloved face still
had the power to divert her from all her good intentions
to remain impervious to him. She'd seen love and pain
written all over that face, laughter and tears, understanding and bewilderment. For her it had shown the deep
hole their relationship had become—a place where they
couldn't talk to each other. Ironic when she remembered

how often Ben used to tease her about how much she
yakked his ear off.

This wasn't getting her any peace from those memories. 'I like your friends from Sydney.'

'You and Rita hit it off fairly quickly.'

'Does that make you uncomfortable?' she asked.

'Why should it?'

'We might talk about you,' she teased, desperate for
light and carefree, not deep and meaningful.

'You'll fall asleep in the first five minutes,' he told
her. 'I heard you and Rita planning a shopping expedition. You've already been indulging your shoe fetish, if
those red ones you wore tonight are anything to go by.'

So he'd noticed her footwear. Did that mean he remembered kissing her toes after removing her beautiful white lace wedding shoes on their wedding night? *I
won't glance his way for fear he does remember every
last little detail.* 'It wouldn't be much of a fetish if I
didn't buy shoes in France.' Two pairs were only the
beginning. She had plenty of time to source more beautiful creations. And buy a second case to take her pur-
chases home.

'Have you really kept up with my career?'

'I haven't been stalking you, but I knew when you
qualified from Sydney Hospital.' She'd first heard it on
the grapevine at work. Because Ben had left under a big,
black cloud, his name had still been gold for the gossips.
'I read an article about the clinic you work for in London and you were mentioned. I never knew you wanted
to move to the UK.'

'I wouldn't have if my original career plans hadn't
been derailed.' His voice darkened, and he looked out towards the sea as if he couldn't bear to let her see his face.

Light and carefree just blew away. Guess that was

always going to happen when they got together, only she wasn't ready. Would she ever be? 'I cared about what you did, where you went.' She drew a breath. 'You had great plans for your career and it bothered me that you might lose sight of them after what happened.'

'Those plans were what kept me going at times, even if they were somewhat altered.' The sadness was rolling off him in waves. Seemed his emotions were all over the place, too.

Tori wanted to hug him. Not that she would. That'd only lead to misunderstandings. Thank goodness some grains of sense remained in her brain. 'I'm glad you've done so well. Truly glad. You deserved a second chance.'

'You think?' Doubt imbued his question.

'Yes, I do. Always have, what's more.' She spun around to stare at him, saw when caution registered in his eyes, replacing that sadness. She'd touched on the taboo subject when she'd sworn she wouldn't. What made her think they could talk about it now when they hadn't been able to at the time they'd been living through it? 'It was the same for me. The work keeping me on the straight and narrow, I mean.' She grimaced. 'Sorry, let's drop this.' So much for light and happy.

'It's as though we haven't moved on, as if the last seven years add up to nothing, great careers notwith-standing. There's this enormous block in the way of even having an everyday conversation.' He'd stopped walking and now stood looking at her. 'Do you want to finish your walk alone?' The loneliness in his voice wrapped around her heart.

'No,' she whispered. 'No. I'd like to catch up a bit. I promise to stick to safe topics.'

Ben remained absolutely still, just watching her. If she hadn't known better she'd almost think he cared something for her. But she did know better. He'd left her. Told her it was over and packed his bags, his explanation leaving a lot to answer for.

Help. What could she say to him that would make him relax? Nothing came to mind. Her mind was blank. For so long she'd wanted the opportunity to ask Ben the real reason he'd left her; why he hadn't wanted to tell her his side of what had happened that day in Theatre that had cost his patient's life and put his future in jeopardy; or had he stopped loving her as easily as he'd made out? Except he'd never said precisely that, she realised with a shock. Only hinted at it. But now it was too late, and any answers wouldn't change a thing. They'd both moved on, created new lives, and now, at this very moment, she had to make light conversation.

Slowly she turned and continued walking, suddenly afraid he'd leave her to go back to the hotel. She wanted him with her. *Why?* She had no idea, only knew that she hadn't had enough time with him yet. She held her breath until he finally joined her. They walked in silence for a few minutes, then Tori said, 'Tell me what your brother's been up to lately.'

'Adam's married to a woman who keeps him in line, and he loves every minute of it. They have two beautiful little girls who I get to see a couple of times a year when they come to London.'

'Bet they adore Uncle Ben,' she managed to gasp out as her stomach cramped. On their first date he'd told her he wanted children one day. If only he knew how close they'd come to being parents. Again her finger rubbed the bracelet. She'd kept a secret from Ben when she shouldn't have. This was a minefield. Not talking at all was awkward, but discussing everyday stuff exposed other issues that had festered over the years.

'Of course.' Ben smiled softly, like he had a store of memories in his mind of his nieces. After a moment, he asked quietly, 'Are you in a relationship?'

'No, I'm not. Most men I meet prefer a woman who comes home at the same time every night and cooks dinner and entertains them.' No man had the ability to turn her bones to syrup with just a look. No man except the one walking beside her.

'You're looking in the wrong places.'

I'm not looking. Another change of subject was needed—fast. 'Tell me about working in Sydney. You worked with some wonderful surgeons. I wondered if you might've stayed on there to set up your own clinic.' That had to be safe, hadn't it?

'You really did keep up with my career.'

'Of course I did.' She hadn't been able to help herself. 'Knowing how fantastic you were at what you did I couldn't bear the thought you mightn't achieve your dreams.' Why had she said that out loud? Ben didn't need to know she'd still cared enough to follow his career, or that she'd been breaking up inside, thinking he'd lost his chance at success because of what had happened in Auckland. She still wanted to know all the details of that botched operation, but not once had he told her a thing, so the chances of him telling her were now zilch.

'You and me both. But…' He hesitated. Wondering how far to take this conversation? It was a little too close and personal, considering where their relationship was. 'Moving to Sydney turned out to be a good decision.'

It must've been difficult, starting afresh with a malpractice issue against his name. 'I'm glad you see it like that.'

He shrugged. 'Not a lot of choice. I was given a second chance. Of course I grabbed it.' He paused before saying, 'Working in a different environment opened my eyes to the fact that a department could be run very successfully without a domineering man like my father at the helm.'

'He did have a reputation for great work.' Tori shuddered. And bull-minded tactics for getting exactly what he wanted.

Ben nodded. 'Sure, he did. But he could've achieved that without being so dictatorial.'

Who was this Ben? The man she'd married hadn't done talking about important things, had never criticised his father. *Ben always told you how much he loved you.* Okay, that had been important.

Tori sighed. Why was she even thinking about the past? Their marriage was well and truly over. Right now all she wanted to do was enjoy being in France and having some fun for a change. Fun that didn't, shouldn't, include Benji.

Torture. Walking beside Tori, not touching, was pure torture. Listening to her voice, seeing the animation coming and going in her face whenever she turned his way. Definitely torture. Ben fought the need to wrap an arm around Tori's shoulders, to feel her move under his grasp. That would be for himself, not for her. She wouldn't appreciate the action. He'd been kidding himself to think he'd be able to see her and walk away unscathed. How could he when he still had deep feelings for her? Feelings he would not be acting on. Loneliness fired up, trampled on his heart.

He'd only ever felt this alone once before—when he'd left Tori. Now he was with her and nothing had changed. He dragged air into his lungs. Warm sea air from the Mediterranean. Tori must be beside herself about being here. 'So you're going to Paris after this?' When she nodded, he asked, 'Are you one of those Monsieur Leclare has asked to repeat your talk at the medical school?'

'Yes. Are you?'

He nodded. 'I'm replacing my colleague, who couldn't make it.' Then, 'I'm looking forward to hearing you speak tomorrow.'

Her shoulders tensed for a moment. 'I'm as nervous as I've ever been.'

'Get away with you. It'll be a walk in the park.' Tori had never had a problem with talking, one on one or in a group.

'Thanks for the vote of confidence.' Her smile was tender, and untied one of the knots deep within him—knots that had been there since that fateful day when his world had come crashing down at his feet.

He nodded. 'Why the nerves? Haven't you prepared enough?' Of course she would've. This was the woman who studied harder than anyone else and treated everything she did with fierce intensity. Including their marriage. *Including their divorce.*

'Why do you think Monsieur Leclare invited me to give a talk on rheumatic fever and the resulting heart disease?'

'Because you're becoming quite the expert.' Word was getting around about the cardiologist in New Zealand who'd set up a clinic to help the children who'd got heart problems after having rheumatic fever. According to the conference notes everyone had received, Tori had become known as the Heart Lady. 'You're saving children from ever appearing in our operating theatres.'

'On the scale of cardiac things, I'm small fry. I'm not making groundbreaking discoveries, or coming up with new procedures.' She sounded so perplexed he wanted to hug away her doubt.

'What you do is equally important. You wait. I bet you get a standing ovation.' He'd start one if no one else did.

'Don't overdo it.' She chuckled, a soft, warm sound that lightened his heart, and undid another knot.

Keep this up and he'd soon be like a floppy piece of string, all tension gone. He held a splayed hand against his chest. 'She wounds me.'

Another of those chuckles had him thinking if only he could make her repeat them all the way back to the hotel. 'Time we turned back? We are getting into a less populated area.'

Tori stopped to look around. 'You're right.' Then she yawned. 'Seems the day has finally caught up with me.'

Ben took a chance and lifted her hand to tuck it on his arm, then headed back the way they'd come, enjoying the way her hip nudged him as she walked and desperately hoping she wouldn't pull away. Diversionary tactics might work. 'How's Molly?'

'Mum's awesome. She's playing golf three days a week, has joined a chess club and is playing bridge. She sold the house to move into a retirement village last year.'

'No way. Not Mrs Independence.' He'd got on well with Tori's mother. She took no nonsense from anyone, not even him. He'd missed her a lot.

'Says it's the best decision she's made in a long time. Personally I don't get it, but it's her call. I can hardly start telling her how to live her life when she's always backed me in everything I've done, whether it was the right or wrong thing to do.'

'She's very wise, your mum.' Wonder what Molly had

to say about him these days? He'd gone to see her once when everything had been falling apart and received only kindness, though she'd said nothing that would put Tori in a bad light. She was a good mother, made all the more so because she'd brought Tori up alone after her husband had been killed in a trucking accident when Tori had been a nipper.

Tori tightened her fingers on his arm for a moment, and he waited to hear what she'd come out with next. But she must've changed her mind because that grip loosened and she remained quiet.

What would she say if he gave in to the need crawling through him and took her in his arms to kiss her? Why ask? He knew the answer. She'd slap him down and avoid him like the plague for the rest of the conference. Tori had never lacked common sense.

'Have you met anyone else that you're serious about?' Tori suddenly turned his question from earlier back on him.

When he glanced at her she was staring straight ahead, tension tightening her throat. 'No. There's never a lot of time for relationships. I remember how hard it was for you and I to have together time.' They'd been like ships in the night at times.

'That's a little different. I was studying and we were both putting in horrendous hours in the department.'

'True.' Given he'd married the love of his life and that had failed, what hope did any other relationship have? None, when he hadn't quite laid that first one to rest yet. Hopefully the next few days would see to that.

They reached the sweeping entrance to the hotel and Ben led Tori inside to the elevators. Chancing a light kiss on her cheek, he inhaled her scent of roses. 'Goodnight, Tori. See you in the morning.'

She entered the elevator and pressed the number for her floor. As the doors slid shut he saw her raise her fingers to the spot he'd just kissed.

Goodnight, Tori, he repeated silently to himself. *You were the love of my life. Now you're Tori, ex love of my life.*

He needed to keep reminding himself of that.

'Want a nightcap?' John asked from behind him.

'That's the best idea you've had all day.' It might be the thing to send him to sleep later, because at the moment it looked like being a very long night. 'Where's Rita?'

'Tucked up in bed, planning her shopping expedition with Tori.' John rolled his eyes. 'Women, eh? What is it about shops that gets their knickers in such a twist?'

'French shops, man, not just any shops.' He'd love to take Tori shopping, spoil her with jewellery and more stylish dresses like the one she'd worn tonight. It had fitted her tall, lithe figure to perfection, reminding him of every curve he'd loved nothing more than to kiss and caress until she'd cried out and begged him for release. 'Better make that whiskey a triple.'

CHAPTER THREE

TORI PICKED UP the phone in her room. 'Hello?'

'Hey, it's me.'

Under her satin robe her nipples peaked at the sound of that deep timbre. 'Good morning, Ben.' At least she hadn't said Benji. She held her breath as she waited to see why he'd rung, trying to ignore the pitter-pattering of her heart. This odd rhythm was new to her repertoire of reactions to all things Benji. Ben. The pattering got louder.

'I'm thinking breakfast at one of those street cafés would be a great start to the day. Want to join me? All part of not spending any more time than necessary in the hotel.'

How could she turn that down? 'Sounds lovely. Meet you downstairs in twenty.'

'Twenty it is.'

Breakfast with Ben. In a street café in Nice. That had to be the best way ever to start a day.

Yeah, yeah, don't let it go to your head. He is still Ben and you are still no longer his other half.

He didn't have another half. Neither did she. But that didn't mean they'd be joining up again.

Just keep things on an even keel and don't let that voice trip you up.

Easy as. Be friendly and cool. Easy as.

A little while later Tori sniffed the air like a spaniel on the scent of a bone. They'd walked up Avenue Jean Médecin until they'd found a patisserie with seating on the pavement. The delicious scent of pastries teased her. 'Look at those.' She nodded at the array of exquisitely presented delicacies. 'This is heaven.' She grinned.

'You want to try out your French and order for both of us?' He grinned straight back.

'Woo-hoo. Yes, I do. What are you going to have?' Anticipation rolled through her, egged on by that smile beaming at her. *Oh, Ben, I've missed you.* She wouldn't be sad today. That'd be a waste of Nice. Stepping up to the counter, she pulled back her shoulders and said slowly and carefully, *'Un café, un café au lait, et deux pains au chocolat, s'il vous plaît.'* She handed over a twenty-euro note to the taciturn woman behind the counter and watched closely to see what she got.

'Sucre?' she was asked.

'Non.' Who'd have believed she'd be ordering breakfast in French? She glanced around and met Ben's laughing eyes.

'It's looking good so far. That's two coffees on the go.' He sounded as happy as her.

Pulling a face at him, she chuckled. 'Ye of little faith.' And mentally crossed her fingers they got one white and one black.

When their order was placed on the counter Tori grinned as she handed Ben his. 'I did it. I got what we wanted without having to utter a single word in English.' She hadn't had so much fun since—since she and Ben had been married and sharing the apartment.

Her excitement faded a little as they sat outside, but she refused to give in to the past and instead watched the trams rolling up and down the centre of the avenue, stopping for workers to alight. Tourists wandered by, some stopping to peer in the window at the food on offer.

'I could get to like doing this all the time.' The sky was clear blue again, the temperature already warming up. 'Thanks for suggesting it.'

'Like you said, why sit in the hotel dining room when Nice is out here? When France is spread before us to enjoy?'

Tori nodded her agreement. 'Even if I'd got green juice and a baked banana from my badly accented order I'd have been happy. This is what I came all this way for.'

'Don't tell Luc. He'd be disappointed.' Ben's smile struck her right in the solar plexus, dissolving the last of the tension his sudden appearance yesterday had created.

Not even the child bouncing on the seat at the next table and poking her tongue out at Tori could dampen her spirits with thoughts of what her child would've been like at that age.

'This is the first holiday I've had in ages. Or it will be once my talk is done.' If she remained practical hopefully this little frisson of interest in Benji would go away. *Ben. His name is Ben.*

Tori waited for the applause that followed Monsieur Leclare's introduction to die down. It was show time. She felt good, knew her stuff, had all the notes printed out just in case her phenomenal memory failed her—as if. The PowerPoint display was set up and she'd tested it with a technician fifteen minutes earlier. Yes, she was ready.

When the forum director waved her forward to the lectern she stepped up and looked out across the crowded conference room. And forgot everything. Except that she was there to talk to all those people. Her mouth dried. The notes shook in her fingers. She glanced down at them. Nothing made sense. What was going on? This had never happened before. The room was quiet. Too quiet. Her gaze slid down and along the front row. To Ben. Don't look at Ben. What can he do? Where else did she look? No way could she cope with seeing all those expectant faces turned to her, those eyes focused entirely on her. Try the screen. Spinning around like a desperate woman—which she was—she studied the heading blinking out at the audience.

Rheumatic Fever and Its Comeback by Tori Wells. Cardiologist, New Zealand

That should've settled her stage fright. It didn't. Instead, the quivering increased and her stomach got in on the act, preparing to hurl that delicious pastry upward.

A firm voice cut across her panic. 'Tori, here are the notes you left behind.' Ben.

Ben was on stage with her, handing her something. Notes. She reached for them as though they were a lifeline. But they couldn't be hers, she had all the notes she needed on the laptop in front of her. It was knowing what to do with them that was the problem.

'Read them.' His expression was filled with confidence.

She glanced down at the top page of what was one of the numerous pads supplied by the hotel for the attendees. Scrawled across the paper in handwriting she remembered well was, *'Speak from your heart, Tori, as only you can.'*

Dared she look at him? Could the whole auditorium hear her rapid heartbeat over the microphone? It was deafening. Was she about to make a colossal fool of herself?

A hand was on her elbow, fingers squeezing gently. 'Go, girl.' A whiff of that aftershave and the hand was gone as Ben walked off stage.

Leaving her to do this. He believed in her. Knew she could speak to all these experts and not screw up. Drawing air into her depleted lungs, she faced forward and said, 'Ladies and gentlemen, I am sure I'm about to tell you things you have known since the first day you walked into medical school, but I believe in my work so much you're going to have to listen to me anyway.'

That got her a laugh. The show was under way. A quick glance at Ben found him nodding and smiling—at her. *I owe you.* The tension fell away and Tori opened up to talk about what had driven her for the last few years.

'I would like you all to meet Thomas Kahu. He needs no introduction. He's the star of this short clip.' She pressed 'Play' and stepped aside so everyone could watch sixty seconds of high-school rugby.

When the film clip finished she returned to the lectern, her nerves completely under control. If Thomas could see her he'd be saying, 'Come on, Heart Lady, they're only people like you and me.' He was one smart young man.

She told her audience, 'I come from a rugby-mad country, but that particular game was the one to change me profoundly. It also changed my career direction.' Her voice firmed as she continued. 'I attended a school rugby game in which my friend's son was playing. There was a big, strapping Samoan lad in the back line of the opposition team who was impressing everyone. Thomas Kahu was a natural at reading the game and acting on what he saw. There was even talk on the evening sports news that night of him being considered for the junior national side in a year or two.' Sadness enveloped her, tightening her heart.

'Three months later that lad was sitting in my consulting room suffering from carditis that manifested as congestive heart failure. He'd contracted rheumatic fever. His rugby career was over before it had really started. Thomas is the reason I do what I do.' The emotion she always felt about that day filled her voice, and was amplified through the microphone.

Some people clapped and Tori felt a glow of pleasure nudge aside her distress for Thomas. Ben had been right. Speak from the heart. Heck, she was just about laying the whole pumping mass out on the lectern for everyone to see.

Now for the nitty-gritty of her everyday life. 'While rheumatic fever is common worldwide, it has been fairly rare in Western countries since the nineteen sixties. But this leaves no room for complacency as there have been some outbreaks since the early eighties.' Tori looked out across the room without focusing on any one person. So far, so good. The delegates were receiving her well.

Straightening her back even farther, she felt a vertebra click as she continued. 'In New Zealand, rheumatic fever has become a small but serious issue for a minority of our population. The health ministry is working hard to put in preventative measures through education, better housing and communal involvement on all levels.

'Unfortunately I get to see far too many children who don't come to anyone's attention until it's too late and they've developed heart disease. This is due in part to the fact that initially parents, teachers and other caregivers believe that when the child becomes ill with a sore throat he or she has an infection and treat it accordingly.

In some instances there's no treatment at all even for a strep throat.'

Sipping water, Tori again looked out at the sea of faces, then inadvertently brought her focus down to the front row. Ben smiled directly at her and gave her a thumbs-up. She smiled back.

'Ignorance is not the answer. Strep A is easily treated with antibiotics and yet this is often overlooked, especially in the lower socio-economic regions of our society where people can't afford even a heavily subsidised visit to the doctor.

'What my clinic is pushing for are standard observations that can be undertaken by trained community nurses at every school in the country. I'd rather run out of young patients with cardiac disease brought on by rheumatic fever than have to perform even one more heart-replacement procedure. I'd prefer to see these kids playing rugby and netball, not dealing with shortness of breath, not terrified because their heart sounds and feels strange. No child wants to be the odd one out, and yet because of the consequences of this disease that's where they often find themselves.'

Her voice had risen and her hands were fists on the lectern as she tried to lock eyes with every single person in the room. 'Kids need to belong, to be a part of what's going on around them. They don't deserve to be sidelined through a preventable illness.'

Someone clapped, and that was quickly followed by the whole room joining in. *Oh, my goodness.*

Waiting for the noise to die down, Tori shifted from foot to foot. *All I'm doing is telling it like it is.* Glancing at her watch, she was astonished to see that twenty minutes had gone by already.

This meant so much to her, had been her life, in some

ways replacing Ben and the baby. Maybe she overdid the workload, but what did that matter if she was helping these children and their families? 'I've seen these children, held their hands, wiped their tears, dulled their pain, encouraged them to get on in life. Sometimes I've sat at their bedsides all night long. These are normal, everyday children who find themselves in a difficult predicament because no one understood that a simple strep throat could go wild.' She had the audience completely. She felt it in the air—as though everyone was holding their breath.

'Then there are the parents. Guilt eats at them, tears them to pieces when they understand what went wrong and how easily it could've been prevented. Trying to tell them it's not their fault does nothing to alleviate their pain. Only education on all levels is going to do that for the next parents who have a sick child.

'Thomas's parents still blame themselves three years on from learning that the same strep throat his sister recovered from quickly had done this to their beloved boy. Even now when Thomas is getting on with his life they're bewildered about how it happened. The point is, it shouldn't have occurred in a modern society such as New Zealand's. And we're not the only Western country dealing with these outbreaks. It is not a disease of the past. It is here, on our doorsteps, doing damage, now.'

She took another sip of water to give her throat time to unblock. 'Next I'm going to discuss three case studies with you.' An usher could've yelled 'Bomb!' and Tori doubted anyone would've heard and, she suspected, not just because many were concentrating on the translators babbling in their earpieces. *Wow. Amazing. I'm doing fine.*

The third case told of the downside of what Tori did

for sick children. She wrapped up with, 'Caroline was too weak to fight the fight needed to save her life. Losing a patient is incredibly hard, but we can't win every battle. I try, believe me, I try. But...' she looked around the auditorium '...medicine isn't perfect and neither are its practitioners.'

Once again she found her gaze drifting down to the front row and Ben. He was watching her with a stunned look on his face, and when their eyes connected he mouthed, 'You're right.'

Tori nodded before saying to the audience, 'To finish, I have one more short clip to show you.' She pressed a button on her laptop and once again the screen filled with kids playing rugby. Only this time Thomas was on the sideline, walking up and down, shouting encouragement to the children.

Tori knew she was smiling as she watched. She was so proud of her patient. At the end she returned to the microphone. 'Thomas now coaches school rugby and this year started training to become a teacher. But for rheumatic fever he might've become an All Black. And, believe me, the French can be relieved he didn't.'

Except for the laughter, it was over. She'd done it, thanks to Ben getting her started.

Monsieur Leclare gave her a kiss on each cheek before turning to the audience. 'That, ladies and gentlemen, is why we invited the Heart Lady to speak to us. Named that by her young patients because they obviously understand how much she cares. She has touched all of us with her sincerity about her patients and her work with them. Today we heard such passion that I believe Madame Tori Wells has reminded each and every one of us of why we are doctors.'

Tori could feel tears backing up in her throat as

everyone stood to clap her off the stage. Tears for
Thomas and all the other youngsters like him. Tears for
not being able to give them back life as they'd known it.

Then Ben stepped in front of her and wrapped his
arms around her. 'That was brilliant. Just brilliant.'

'What a difference twenty-four hours can make.' Ben
watched Tori being waylaid by yet another delegate as
she tried to make her way across the beautifully decorated room in which they were attending the conference cocktail party. Last night she'd been reluctant to
join him; tonight her eyes expressed the desire to reach
him as soon as possible even if only to put space between her and her adoring fans. But she was being gra-
cious, stopping to answer questions and talk to anyone
who waylaid her.

'She's a star,' said Rita. 'That was some talk today.'

'You were there?' Ben couldn't take his eyes off Tori.
That raw emotion in her voice as she'd spoken to the
conference had stayed with him all day. It had been so
genuine it had touched everyone. This was a side to Tori
he hadn't experienced before—or not in such depth.

'John sneaked me in. I wanted to hear what your
Heart Lady was all about, and now I know. She's amazing. Neither is she afraid to admit she doesn't get it right
all the time.'

Yeah, he'd got that message. But, then, he'd not denied his error of judgement, either. He'd told the board
of inquiry, just not his wife. 'No wonder the Wells Heart
Clinic is becoming famous.' Pride mingled with sadness.
Unfortunately Tori was not *his* Heart Lady, but she had
owned his heart. 'She'll never leave New Zealand for a
career elsewhere.'

He didn't realise he'd said that bit out loud until Rita tapped his arm. 'You could always move back home.'

The understanding in her voice nearly undid him. His mixed-up emotions about his ex were private and yet his friends seemed to know exactly what was going on in his head and heart—probably better than he did. But, then, they'd been there the day the divorce had become final, John getting drunk with him and Rita hugging him the next morning and cooking him a hangover-breaking breakfast. *You want closure, remember? Not a rerun.*

Pinching the bridge of his nose, he searched for a neutral subject—anything to get away from Rita's telling comment. 'Have you and Tori hit the shops yet?'

Rita fixed him with wide eyes. 'Excuse me? Aren't I looking stunning?'

He grinned. 'You always do.'

'Cheeky.' Rita swiped his arm. 'Get an eyeful of Tori. That emerald-green sheath was made for her. It's perfect.'

He'd had an eyeful. More than one. He hadn't been able to stop staring from the moment he'd seen her enter the room. The dress was superb, again defining her height, highlighting all her curves and emphasising the colour of those sparkling eyes. Tonight she'd let her hair fall loose over her shoulders, the many shades of red gleaming under the lights. She looked good enough to eat.

Ben sighed. Unfortunately he wasn't the only one waiting impatiently to talk to her. At the rate this was going he'd get to say hello about the time the cocktail party wrapped up.

'We could go snaffle her,' Rita said.

He'd like nothing better. He also didn't want to get on the wrong side of her when so far today they'd managed get along without any hiccups. 'What? Spoil her night? I don't think so.'

'Wise man.' John added his euro's worth. 'How about we four go out to a restaurant after this shindig's over?'

'I'd like that.' But would Tori?

'Ask her.' Rita nudged him, obviously having picked up on his doubt. 'When you get a chance.'

'She is kind of popular, isn't she?' Ben felt another wave of pride blitz him. The big thing to come out of that talk, apart from her passion, was that she really didn't know how much she'd touched everyone. Or if she did she was very circumspect about it. But, hey, this was Tori, the girl who'd never forced her opinions on anyone. The one time he'd thought she'd been going to, he'd shut her down before a word had got out and landed between them like a grenade with the pin pulled. How would their lives, their marriage have turned out if he had listened? If he'd sat down and told her everything, especially how he'd been thinking of the kudos he'd get from his colleagues and pride from his father when he successfully did a procedure until then untried in New Zealand and which had resulted in his patient's death? He would never know what she'd thought. His shame had ruled. He hadn't wanted to see the disdain enter her eyes, hadn't wanted her to think him less than the best at his work.

John waved over a waitress laden with a very full tray of wine and champagne. 'Rita? Ben?'

'I'm in France. Champagne is the only way to go.'

'Me, too,' Ben told him.

As Ben lifted his glass to his lips he glanced across to Tori again and met her full-on look. *Rescue required* seemed to blink out at him over the sudden gap in the crowd. They'd always done that for each other at functions they'd had to attend with his parents.

'Here, hold mine, will you?' He thrust the glass at John. 'I'll be back.'

He reached Tori as two eminent surgeons from New York started asking her questions about the surgery she performed. 'Hey.' He leaned close to her and tucked an arm around her waist. When she tensed he didn't move, waiting for her to relax again.

One of her fans jerked his head around to stare at him as though he was an interloper. Couldn't fault that. He was, in a way. 'Benjamin Wells, isn't it? From London?' The guy thrust a hand forward. 'Adrian Packer, senior cardiologist.' He named one of the most well-known hospitals in the United States, sounding as though there really was no other hospital to be working at. 'Your wife certainly set us back on our butts today, reminding us about grassroots medicine like that.'

My wife? Yeah, well. Relieved he hadn't acted badly before Adrian had had his say, Ben shook the extended hand with warmth. 'Tori has a way of doing that.'

Her head twisted around and her chin came up as she stared at him. 'I do? Why, thank you, Mr Wells.' Then she turned back to the two men, who looked like they could stay talking to her all night. 'Would you mind dreadfully if I joined Ben and our friends for a while? I don't wish to be rude, but I'm feeling overwhelmed with all the attention.'

Adrian smiled in an avuncular way. 'Of course, my dear. I'm sure your husband is envious of all the attention you're getting.'

Ben saw her mouth open to refute the husband part of that statement and he tapped her waist to shut her up. These two were being kind, letting her off the hook, but learn that he wasn't her husband and she might be stuck with them for hours. She got the hint and let him lead her away before she felt obliged to say anything else and get caught up in conversation again.

Then she frowned at him. 'Thanks for saving me. I'm sorry everyone seems to think we're married. If it's causing you any problems I'll make sure word gets around that we're divorced.'

His heart knocked painfully against his ribs. Funny but he didn't care that people might think they were husband and wife. 'You going to wear a sign around your neck?'

There must've been something in his voice that gave him away because Tori stopped and turned to stare at him. 'Ben?'

He didn't like the worry flaring in her eyes or the 'we definitely aren't married any more' look—even when it was true and he had no intention of changing the situation. But for some inexplicable reason it rankled. 'Come on. John and Rita are waiting for us.'

He still had to ask if she'd like to join them for dinner. His chances of her saying yes had probably gone down the tube.

But he hadn't counted on Rita. After the women had swapped compliments on the results of their shopping expedition, which they were wearing, Rita quietly slipped in, 'Tori, John and I found a delightful restaurant on our first night here and we're keen to go there again. Would you like to join us after this is over and make a foursome?'

She's going to say no, Rita. Ben held his breath and stared at an interesting spot on the floor.

'That'd be lovely. You are talking French food, aren't you?' Tori's voice lightened.

'Is there any other?' Rita drained her glass and gave Ben a wink over the rim.

He swallowed a laugh and looked for a waiter. 'Tori, would you like a sparkling water?'

'Please.' Coolly spoken.

Still not completely back onside, then. Ben shrugged. That was okay. Dinner would be enjoyable and friendly with John and Rita there to keep the jokes and conversation rolling along. Hopefully by the end of the evening Tori would've got past this little hiccup in their oddball relationship.

'Good, that's sorted.' Rita opened her handbag and pulled out her phone. 'Tori, let me bore you with photos of our kids.'

Tori stiffened, gulped her water, then deliberately dropped her shoulders and leaned closer to Rita. 'They're gorgeous.' She blinked, twice. 'How old are they?'

Ben was fascinated with her reaction. Tori loved children. After all, she'd specialised in caring for them. They'd even talked about having their own family one day. He wondered whether Tori was worried that she might never have kids now. At thirty-six, her biological clock was probably ticking. Loudly, in fact. He winced. Not a lot he could do to help her out.

Dinner didn't eventuate. No one had realised just how many plates of canapés were circulating the room, all too delicious to ignore.

After two hours Rita said, 'I couldn't eat dinner now. How about we go to the restaurant tomorrow night?'

Ben agreed. 'Sounds good to me. The conference winds up late tomorrow afternoon so we'll be left to our own devices anyway.'

Tori had relaxed. 'To be honest, I'm exhausted. I'd have been a wet blanket at dinner. If we can sneak away

I think I'll go for a stroll along the promenade, get some fresh air.'

Rita's eyes lit up and Ben had to swallow his disappointment. He'd been planning on asking Tori to take a walk with him—alone.

Rita said, 'John and I have been ready to leave for a while now.' She nudged John. 'Haven't we, darling?'

'Been counting the minutes.' The look of pure love John gave his wife twisted a knife in Ben's heart.

Lucky man. It was obvious where those two were headed, and it wasn't along the promenade. 'See you in the morning.'

Tori gave Rita a hug. 'Thanks for the shopping.'

Ben watched as John wrapped an arm around Rita's waist and tucked her close while whispering in her ear.

Envy gripped Ben. *I had that once—with Tori.* Then anger replaced the envy. *We threw it away. Both of us. What fools. What stupid, idiotic fools. Especially me. I could've found another way to cope with everything, allowed her closer and told her the whole sordid story, not just parts of it.*

He strode towards the entrance, intent on getting away from people, but it wasn't easy, with the crowd beginning to move in the same direction. It seemed everyone had a similar idea of hitting the promenade. As he waited impatiently to slip through the throng of people he felt a hand on his upper arm.

'Ben? Are you going for a walk?'

He turned to Tori, growled, 'That's where I'm headed, if I ever get out of here.' He turned back, ignoring the blink of shock on her face.

Her hand no longer touched him. He felt the loss immediately and glanced over his shoulder to see Tori pushing in the opposite direction. Her head was held high and that hair spilled down almost to her waist. Her shoulders were so tight they had to be aching.

'Hell.' He swore some more under his breath and followed her, finally catching up as she sank onto a chair at the table they'd all vacated less than five minutes ago.

As she reached for the bottle of water he lightly touched her shoulder. Yep, the muscles under that dress were tight enough to snap. 'Tori, I'm sorry. I shouldn't have barked at you.'

'Why not? It's no more than I deserve for thinking you might want to spend time with me. It's not as though we're together any more. Sometimes over these two days I've found it hard to believe we let it go, you know?' She didn't look at him, instead concentrated on pouring some water into a glass. Most of the liquid spilled onto the table.

He couldn't believe what she'd just admitted. But he wouldn't be fooled into thinking there was a chance of a reconciliation. Tori had to be talking friendship, not full-on love. The problem with that was that reconciliation was not closure. He pulled out another chair and straddled it. Took the bottle and filled the glass for her. 'Yes, I do know what you mean.'

'This whole scenario is...' she shrugged eloquently '...strange.' She raised the glass to her lips.

Strange wasn't a word he'd have used, more like tricky, but she'd got her sentiment across. 'How would you like it to be between us?'

Tori spluttered into the water, wiped her mouth with an abandoned napkin lying on the tabletop. A bright shade of pink flowed into her cheeks as her gaze settled on a spot on the table. 'If I said friends, that seems too insignificant, yet what else can we be? I'm trying not to think about it.'

'You're fibbing.'

She still didn't look at him. 'I know.'

Removing the glass from her shaky grasp, he wrapped his hand around her fingers and stood up, bringing her to her feet beside him. 'Come with me along the Quai. I'd like some quiet time—with you.'

Her head lifted and those eyes that he used to get lost in locked with his. Deep emerald pools that sucked him in and wrapped a layer of warmth around his thawing heart. Eyes that reminded him of things he shouldn't want ever again, was afraid to risk having again. Tori probably didn't know it but her gaze twisted his gut and brought all the love and need he'd known for her charging through his head, his heart and his soul. So much for getting over her.

For the life of him, he could not release her hand.

Tori said softly, 'Let's go.' Then she waited for him to take the first step.

A move that seemed to take minutes to eventuate. Finally he took a step, brought her close, tucked her against him, his arm around her shoulders, and led her out into the warm night air.

They didn't talk all the way to their turning point. Once there Tori sank down onto a bench and tugged her shoes off. 'These are killing me.'

'I'm not surprised.' The heels were unbelievably high. He joined her, leaned back and stretched his legs out in front of him.

'You don't swagger like you used to.' She was grinning at him. To soften the blow? Or to lighten their mood?

Unfortunately, her comment wasn't funny. 'That got knocked out of me.'

Her grin died. 'Tell me about the hearing.'

The air whooshed out of his lungs. He was on his feet in an instant, slamming his hand through his hair. He spun around hard, stared down at her. 'You didn't come. I wanted you there.' *Needed you with me. Needed to know you'd stand by me no matter what the outcome.* 'Even when I didn't want you to know the truth about my error of judgement.'

'You insisted I stay away.'

'You were meant to see through that and come anyway.' He'd tried to have this discussion back then but hadn't been able to find the words without dumping too much of his shock and resentment at what had happened onto her.

Tori nodded. 'I thought as much.' She stared out to sea, her fingers twisting the bracelet she wore. 'I arrived late. I'd been in Theatre and the operation ran overtime.'

'So you did turn up. I never knew that.' They hadn't done a lot of talking in the following weeks when he'd been on stand-down from the hospital and dealing with the hearing, and virtually none at all after he'd packed his bags and walked out of the apartment nearly three months later.

'I tried to tell you, but…'

Tori didn't have to finish that sentence. He'd been intent on keeping his distance to save from telling her what a fool he'd been.

She shrugged, not looking at him. 'By the time I got there the door was shut and I wasn't allowed in.'

'It was a closed session with the hospital board chairman, the ethics committee chairperson and the heads of two other departments.' Not the head of his department. Dad had been furious at being cut from the hearing, too. He'd wanted to manipulate the outcome so his son came out without a blemish.

'So I wouldn't have been allowed to sit in on proceedings.'

'No, but I wanted you there.' He'd have been pleased if he'd known she'd been outside, waiting for him. Except she hadn't waited, had been nowhere in sight when he'd finally come out, many hours later, a changed man. He'd wondered if she hadn't loved him enough to be there for him. What else had he got wrong?

'I sat outside for most of the day, then got called into surgery at the wrong time.'

Ben grimaced. 'I didn't know that, either.' Not that anyone would've told him. He'd become persona non grata by then. Except Tori should've told him. But they had already been shutting off from each other.

Tori looked over, her gaze contrite. 'I'm sorry.'

'Thanks.' He wanted to ask why she'd thought he was guilty when she hadn't had the facts, but he also didn't want to have her withdraw from him right now. Of course she knew now what had happened. Everyone did. It was on record. But he hadn't had the guts to tell her first.

Tori reached for his hand, shuffled closer and didn't let go of him. 'I am glad the hearing was open-minded and allowed that mistakes do happen.'

'So am I.' He couldn't imagine what he'd be doing now if he'd been struck off the register. 'I wouldn't have made a good waiter.'

Her smile was soft and caring, her thumb caressing the back of his hand. 'You'd be great at it, but what a waste.'

'You say the nicest things.' He squeezed her hand and stood up. 'It's cooling down and you just shivered. We'd better make tracks. Barefoot?'

'Until I reach the hotel anyway.' Tori was quiet all

the way back. At the hotel entrance she slipped into her shoes before turning to him. 'I'm glad it worked out for you. I'm very sorry the outcome wasn't the same for us.' Then she was gone, her skirt swirling around her legs as she raced inside and headed for the elevators. *So am I, Tori, love. So am I.* Ben watched until the doors slid shut behind her. *But what's done is done.*

He crossed the reception area, heading for the bar. A nightcap was needed.

CHAPTER FOUR

Jeffery Wells stood close to Tori, leaning over her. 'Talk some sense into Ben. He needs me to get him through this fiasco so he can come out clean.'

She glared at her father-in-law. 'Don't you think this is Ben's decision to make?'

'You want him to ruin his career?' Jeffery slammed back at her.

'That's not what I said.'

'Of course not. You think Ben should take the rap for someone else's irresponsible behaviour.'

'But Benji—' If Benji wasn't responsible for the woman's death, then who was?

Anger and pain sliced through Tori. She rolled over and blinked her eyes open. 'Ben?'

She reached her arm across the wide bed. He wasn't there. He'd be sitting in the lounge, as usual, staring into space.

Tori sat up, startled at how dark the room was. Fumbling at the bedside table, she found the light switch. Soft light spilled into the room. The hotel room in Nice. Not her bedroom back in the apartment.

She'd had a nightmare. A very graphic one with all the details there in vivid colour. Jeffery had been real. The way he'd tried to dominate her by standing over her had been true to form. His harsh words had battered her, as they had that night he'd bowled into the apartment to tell her what she should be doing with Ben, and made her shudder even now she understood she'd been dreaming. Her father-in-law had hated her for standing up to him.

Tossing aside the cover, she leapt out of bed and crossed to haul the heavy curtains open. Then she took a bottle of water from the small fridge and, snapping the lid off, glugged the water straight down.

It hadn't been her place to *tell* Ben what to do. He'd had to make his own decisions about his future, but she'd have talked it through with him anytime he'd wanted. If she'd told Benji his father had pressured her, the chances were that Benji would've shrugged his shoulders and said, 'That's just Dad's way.'

Sure it was. 'Dad's way' had been to rule with an iron will and woe betide anyone who dared to challenge him. Ben adored his father and had spent his life trying to make him proud. It had been like an endless mountain with each achievement shrugged away with the demand for the next goal to be set.

Jeffery's demands of her that day had been pointless. Ben hadn't talked to her. Not about the death of his patient anyway. Heck, by then he'd barely asked if the power bill had been paid any more. It seemed their marriage had been about the good times, and that they hadn't had a clue on handling the bad ones.

Sitting by the window, her legs tucked under her backside, Tori gazed out at the sea, and closer in the promenade, which was devoid of people. Four o'clock. Too early and too dark to go for a brisk walk that'd clear her head.

Was Ben sound asleep? Sprawled on his back, taking

up most of the bed, like he always had? Or had he learned to lie on one side?

Oh, Ben, I loved you so much. We had it all. Or so we thought.

Why had it gone so wrong? They could blame the death of Ben's patient, but if their love had been as strong as she'd believed it to be, they'd have found a way to deal with that. She'd naively thought that if she loved Ben enough they'd never have insurmountable problems, that love conquered everything.

How did other couples cope? Her mother had never remarried after Dad had been killed so she'd not seen first-hand how Mum might've dealt with a crisis in her relationship. Ben's parents had always appeared to have a strong marriage with no hint of dissension, but his mother had tended to take a compliant role.

Last night, talking with Ben, had felt almost like old times. Almost. At the back of her mind a little niggle had kept her aware of how untrue that was, but when he'd wrapped his arm around her shoulders to walk her back to the hotel she'd come close to believing the past had been a nightmare that she'd finally woken up from.

Ben. Benji. Her heart tightened. It was like she hadn't got over him at all. Almost as though she would walk back into her marriage without a backward glance given half a chance.

No way. She'd never go through all that agony again. Watching Ben walk out their front door for the last time had decimated her. It had been as though he'd taken a sledgehammer and pummelled her heart flat.

She leapt up to prowl around the room, looking for a distraction. Her phone lay on the bedside table. Snatching it up, she checked for texts and emails. No texts. Nine emails, mostly from work. Good. They'd keep her busy. And her mind off Ben.

Clicking on the email headed 'Dean Cox', Tori smiled at the cheeky-faced youngster dressed in street clothes and walking out of the clinic's entrance, waving happily. Only weeks ago his health had been deteriorating, despite aspirin treatment for his heart inflammation, and she'd had no choice but to operate, inserting an assist device into his left ventricle to support his blood flow. That had been five days before she'd come away, and every day she'd checked in with her clinic staff to see how Dean was responding.

That photo said it all really. Dean would never be as robust as he'd been before the rheumatic fever had struck, but he was looking a lot better than she'd ever seen him.

Tori tapped in Dean's email address.

Hey, young man, you're looking awesome. Love that T-shirt, by the way.

The T-shirt read 'I'm allowed to be noisy... I'm a kid'.

Bet Mum and Dad don't. ☺ Make sure you come and see me the moment I get home, won't you?
Hugs, the Heart Lady.

Dean would have an appointment already arranged to see her but she liked her kids to know she was there for them anytime, that they always mattered to her. Dean and his parents had walked into her consulting room late one day and told her they'd come from Dunedin to see her because they'd heard the Heart Lady loved her patients so much.

Dean, with his huge eyes and cheeky grin, had stolen into her heart right from that moment. He was one brave little guy who had taken everything she'd told him, and had done to him, as though it had been easy, which it most certainly hadn't been. He'd never complained about life being unfair, never cried—which had worried her sometimes. The counsellor had seen him and come away smiling, saying he was the most together kid she'd ever met. His family had never returned home down south, instead finding jobs and a home in Auckland.

Tori tapped in a reminder to herself to buy T-shirts for all her current patients. She had a list of sizes filed with her emails. A third bag would be needed for her return trip. What would they think at the border when she declared dozens of shirts and zillions of pairs of shoes?

The sun was shoving the night aside by the time Tori had done with answering her mail so she dressed in track pants and a T-shirt, grabbed the city map and went out for a fast walk.

Turning left, Tori headed for Quai Rauba Capeu and the hill overlooking Port Nice on the other side. The steps she found leading directly to the top were gut-busters and she was glad of the challenge. It kept her focused—and out of breath most of the way.

'Wow.' She sighed as she stared down into the port when she finally made it to the edge on the far side of the hilltop.

'Worth those steps, isn't it?' a young man acknowledged in heavily accented English as he jogged past.

A yacht, if anything so large and opulent could really be called a yacht, was tied up to one of the wharves. As she watched two shining black Mercedes-Benz rolled up to the gangway. The uniformed drivers emerged to open the back doors for the four men dressed in suits disembarking.

Tori shook her head in amazement. A very different life from hers, more like something out of a fairytale. And equally unattainable—even if she wanted it, which in all honesty she didn't. But, she sighed again, she could take a day or two of such luxury. Or a week. Or two.

Tearing her gaze away, she looked around for the Monument aux Morts and headed across to study it, before walking along the path to start back down, this time avoiding those steps. She'd find a café for breakfast before going back to the hotel and getting ready for the day.

Ben and his colleagues were first up this morning and she did not want to miss their panel discussion.

Back to Ben. He was never far away, lurking in her mind, waiting to pounce the moment she had nothing else to occupy her.

'Hey, I called to see if you wanted to do breakfast again.' Ben sat down beside Tori in the auditorium. 'Get a better offer?' He smiled to show he held no rancour, though he had been disappointed when she hadn't picked up. Yesterday morning had been fun and he'd wanted to repeat it.

'I went for an early walk.'

When Tori turned to him he saw the dark smudges above her cheekbones. 'You okay?'

'Lack of sleep's catching up.' Her voice was dull, missing yesterday's excitement.

'Got anything to take tonight so you get a good rest?'

'I had a bad dream.' She was staring somewhere beyond his shoulder and looking like she already regretted giving that much information.

'What about?' Tori used to need a bomb under the

bed to wake up. As for nightmares, they had been some-thing other people had, not her. But, then, he hadn't been around lately to know what went on in her life, what might upset her so deeply as to give her bad sleep.

'Your father.'

He barely heard the words, she'd spoken so softly. 'Dad?' A nightmare about his father? Why?

Her abrupt nod told him, yes, definitely.

Why? he repeated to himself, even as something deep and dark began unfurling in his gut. It had taken the malpractice hearing to open his eyes to Dad and see that no amount of hard work and achievement would ever satisfy the old man. That death had occurred partly because he'd been trying to impress Dad, but he'd also wanted the kudos that would've gone with being the first surgeon to use that procedure successfully. If only he hadn't been so cocky and one-eyed. 'What did Dad do?' he asked uneasily.

'He came to apply a little pressure.'

No such thing as a little pressure with the old man. It would've been full-on. 'To do what?' A memory flicked on. There had been a night when he'd come home to get a change of clothes and had seen his father driving away from the apartment. His phone had rung before he'd parked, calling him back to hospital urgently, and by the time he'd had an opportunity to talk to Tori it had seemed unimportant. Had he got that wrong, too?

Ben shifted his butt on the chair, still watching Tori, who lifted her head so he could see directly into those beautiful green eyes that now were apprehensive. He laid a hand on top of hers, which were gripped together on the table. 'Tell me.'

Her eyes widened and she glanced around at the

crowds filling up the seats. 'Not now. You're speaking shortly.'

'Not for an hour. There's been a change to the programme.' He didn't need to hear the first session as much as he needed to know what had caused Tori to look so unhappy. Making a decision, he stood and tugged her gently to her feet. 'Let's get coffee.'

Fully expecting her to refuse, he was relieved when she slung her bag over her shoulder and led the way out and around to a quiet corner in one of the smaller restaurants open for the breakfast rush.

The moment the waitress moved away with their order Tori said, 'I'm so sorry, Ben. I don't know why I told you that. It's not as though I've dreamt about your father before. I guess seeing you after all this time has side effects.' Her smile was lacking in conviction.

Her hand was cold under his. 'Talk to me.'

Tori nodded slowly. 'Jeffery insisted I make you see his way was the best, that you shouldn't take responsibility for that woman's death and should let someone else cop the fallout.'

Ben's stomach sucked in so hard it felt as though it banged against his spine. Nausea swamped him. 'You knew about that, then?'

'Not the details, just the bare minimum.'

'You told Dad to take a hike?' That wouldn't have been easy. Dad could be persistent.

'Obviously.' She locked her gaze with his. 'He told me I'd be ruining your career if I didn't do as he said. But I...' She shrugged. 'You had to make your own decision. What Jeffery or I thought didn't come into it.'

'Thank you. You were right.' No wonder Dad didn't mention Tori's name at all any more. She'd stood up to him far more readily than he had—until then.

'You did the right thing by admitting your error.'

'I agree. But I should've told you everything.' Yet despite him not doing so she'd stood up to his father's threats. He could love her for that alone.

'We weren't doing talking very well by then.' The sadness deepened, turning that emerald green shade of her eyes to something murky. 'It started before your incident in Theatre.'

'Incident?' That was a tame word for what had happened. Though he was pleased Tori wasn't dwelling on how bad that had been or what he'd done.

Another nod. 'Our separation was gradual, had started long before that day, with us working opposing shifts and then studying every spare moment. We swore we knew what we were in for, and that we wouldn't let it happen, but we did. I'd come home from work, have a few drinks to relax me, and then collapse in bed. I was so overwhelmed with the workload at times I'd go to the warehouse outlet to buy up a pile of clothes because I didn't have the energy to do the washing.'

He nodded, found a smile for her. 'You bought me seven T-shirts, each with a day of the week printed on it. You told me you hadn't even looked at anything but the size on the packet.' His smile widened. 'You know something? Sometimes those shirts were the only way I knew what day of the week it was.'

A tear rolled down her cheek. 'It was a fairly hideous time all right. It kind of set us up for what came later, left us unable to deal with it all.'

'Hey.' He picked up a serviette and gently dabbed the tear away. There was nothing Tori could do that would twist his heart more than if she cried. One tear was as good as crying. 'Don't. We're past those months. Look at you with your own clinic and me working in London.

That's why we did all those hours of study and work, to get to where we are now.' At what cost? At the beginning of their marriage they had been unbelievably happy. They'd shared everything from housework to study to intimate dinners, which had often been takeaways because that's all the time or energy they'd had to eat. With hindsight he might get things right second time round. As if there'd be a second time.

'Excuse me, *monsieur, madame.*' The waitress placed two cups of coffee before them.

'*Merci,*' Tori told the girl.

Ben went with, 'Thank you,' and got a smile from Tori. He told her, 'I'm glad you didn't see fit to try and persuade me Dad's way was right. I couldn't have coped with that. I wanted to get it right without any extra pressure about how to go about it.' His stomach slowly returned to normal. But his heart was still having difficulty keeping a regular rhythm. 'I was at fault. That woman would still be alive if not for me wanting to make a name for myself.' There, he'd finally told her. Even if she'd known then, she'd now heard it from him.

About to sip her coffee, Tori gasped and the cup banged back on its saucer. 'None of us can undo anything, Ben. What happened is over and done, and you've moved on. We've moved on. Spending time thinking how differently we could've done things only makes for more distress, not less. I wasn't perfect, either.'

He liked it that she included herself in this; hated it that she truly believed there was no hope for them in the future. Not together, anyway. Tori had moved on. He'd thought he had, too. Seemed he might've got that wrong.

Since when had he begun to think they could still have something going for them anyway?

Since the moment he'd spied her in the crowd, that glorious hair like a beacon beckoning him.

Or had it been when they'd eaten pastries on the street yesterday?

During their walks along the promenade?

Listening to her talk about her young patients at the conference? Yes, maybe, except that's when he'd known her future remained firmly in New Zealand so there was no chance of a relationship together. Long distance didn't cut it, would be far worse than living in the same apartment and hardly seeing each other. He couldn't leave England. Starting his career a third time spoke of unreliability, something he wasn't prepared to be known for. He had to show he could be the surgeon he'd dreamed of becoming. Show himself more than anyone else.

Back in the auditorium Tori barely took in a word Luc was saying to the audience as he introduced Ben and his colleagues for their session. Round and round in her skull went the words Ben had said over coffee.

He'd handled the situation all wrong. Yes, he had, but so had she. He'd never lied to her, just had never given her his version of what had happened, had never sat down with her to have an in-depth talk about how he'd felt and what he'd wanted to do. She still couldn't fathom why he'd left her. That had cut deep.

For Ben to say goodbye after citing their lack of communication and the attention he needed to give his career to get past the stigma created by the death of his patient, which would mean even less time with her, had been hard to swallow. But when he'd added he didn't love her the same any more she hadn't had an answer to that. If love had died, it had died, and there had been no resurrecting it. Or so she'd told herself countless times over the intervening years.

But she hadn't been entirely honest, either. Ben's departure had been a terrible blow, and then she'd had an even bigger shock when she'd lost the baby she hadn't even realised she'd been carrying. By then it had been too late. What good would it have done to tell him she'd lost their baby? Of course, Ben would have come back to help her if she'd asked, but Tori had known she wouldn't be able to cope with the pain of him leaving her a second time. The only reason she'd have accepted Ben back would've been if he loved her, but he'd told her he didn't.

John nudged her. 'It's starting.'

When she looked at Ben's friend she saw concern directed at her and felt guilty for being so rude. She'd barely spoken to him when he'd come and taken Ben's chair at the front to keep her company. 'Thank you.'

John nodded. 'No worries,' he said in true Aussie style.

That made her smile and then she looked up at the stage and gave Ben an even bigger one. Whatever their differences and unresolved issues, she was glad they were having this time together.

Sitting back, Tori listened with growing interest to the four men on stage talking about heart transplant procedures. They came with an established record of success, and with ever-increasing survival rates over the difficult first year after the transplant.

'Which,' Ben pointed out in answer to a question from the floor, 'means increased survival rates in ongoing years.'

'Is the rate any better in transplants using hearts that have to be restarted after death?' Another question from the floor.

'That technique is still in the early stages so we don't yet have enough data to know the answer to that. But I don't see why the outcome can't be as good as with live hearts.'

Ben's enthusiasm for his work was apparent in his voice, his facial expressions and the way he held his body. Tori watched in wonder, transfixed. This was Ben at his best. This was the man she'd known he'd become. Thank goodness the medical council had had the foresight to let him continue his career without intervention.

'Ben's really something, isn't he?' John leaned close as the audience clapped at the end of the session.

'Yes, he is,' she agreed around a blockage in her throat brought on by unshed tears.

'London's lucky to have him.'

Tori raised an eyebrow at the wistful note in John's voice. 'You tried to keep him in Sydney?'

'Absolutely. But he was determined to go halfway round the world and prove he could mix it with the big boys. I don't think that was the real reason at all, as he's not a snob. But something was driving him to go away.'

'I wonder if he wanted as much distance as possible between him and Auckland.' Did John know what had happened there?

John shrugged. 'Listening to him, I can't say he was wrong to go. He's found his niche.'

A chill lifted bumps on her skin. 'You're right. He's never going to move back Down Under. Especially if he gets that partnership he told me he's hanging out for.' The sooner she accepted that, the sooner she could stop thinking about him other than as someone she used to know very well.

'Tori, Ben could do transplants in New Zealand as easily as in London.'

'What are you saying?' Didn't he want Ben back in Sydney?

'He made his mind up to head to England the day your divorce was finalised. Before he got drunker than I've ever seen a man.'

'I don't think you should be telling me that.' *I don't want to know that. It's too late.*

'Ben's my friend. I want what's best for him.' John looked sad as he stood up. 'A wonderful career is all very well, but there are more important things to think about. I've seen him play with my kids, seen his eyes fill with longing for his own family.'

Tori watched John weave his way through the crowd, leaving her to digest what he'd not said. Had Ben gone so far away to put maximum distance between them? That didn't make sense. She hadn't been knocking on his door, asking for a second chance—not since those first bewildering and horrible weeks after he'd walked out on her. Once she'd gone to see him, begging for him to come back or at least explain why he didn't love her any more, but faced with his unwavering stance she'd quickly found her pride and stopped harassing him. Then she'd miscarried and that had been that. No going back.

Had John been suggesting Ben hadn't really wanted to go? Or that he wanted to return? No, not likely. No one had forced him to go. He could've stayed on in Sydney, even returned to Auckland if he'd wanted to. As he could anytime he chose.

More confused than ever, Tori stood up, surprised how the uncertainty confusing her made her legs unsteady. Someone nudged her in passing and she hesitated. Next on the agenda was morning tea and then another session in here.

'Hey, Tori.' She heard Ben's voice over the heads of people pressing to get out of the room. He was pushing against the tide to get to her.

'Hey, Ben,' she whispered.

Suddenly she couldn't do it, had to get outside and away from everyone. Away from where Ben was. She needed to clear her mind of all this and find calm before being able to talk to him as though there was nothing wrong between them. She needed to find strength and resolve so every time she looked Ben in the eye she wouldn't have this crazy urge to pitch herself into his arms and hold on for ever.

She needed to withdraw and regroup. To find a backbone and remain impervious to his charm, friendship and all the things she knew he could be. Loving, sexy, fun, caring…

CHAPTER FIVE

TORI CHARGED OUT of the hotel and through the door held open by the doorman. *'Merci,'* she acknowledged, and took a breath of fresh air.

It had become claustrophobic inside. Hundreds of conference attendees seemed to be pushing against her, taking her air, deafening her with their incessant chatter.

'Madame Wells, are you all right?' Monsieur Leclare was beside her.

'Oui. It's very warm inside and I needed to get some air. That's all.' No way could she tell this kind man she was about to bolt from his conference and go AWOL.

'You've been listening to the panel, no?'

She nodded. 'It was excellent.'

'And yet you are flustered. I think you need time away from all these people.'

Exactly. One in particular. But she wasn't telling Luc that. 'I thought I'd take a short break outside while everyone's having coffee.'

'Non, non. I have an idea. Take a few hours off. You're in Europe, you must see some of the sights.' Before she could agree and tell him she already had plans to study the map and see where she could go to get away from any chance of bumping into Ben, he snapped his fingers at the concierge.

Tori couldn't keep up with his rapid French, and there obviously wouldn't be any chance of her having a say on where she was going so she gave in and waited with interest to see how the rest of her day transpired. This was exactly what she needed—a distraction from Benji. *Ben.* When would she stop thinking Benji?

Less than an hour later Tori found her seat in the train carriage her taxi driver had led her to. Sinking into it, she looked around at her fellow passengers. Tourists hauling heavy backpacks, local women with their shopping bags, elderly couples on an outing. This was one of the regular runs down the coast to the border with Italy, and she had a return ticket for today. Understanding most of what was being spoken was near impossible so she let the talk flow over her, like she was in a cocoon where nothing could touch her. Right now she wanted to absorb France, not stress about anything.

As the train pulled out of the station she turned her focus onto the buildings they passed, let the tension ease out of her muscles. Years back she'd have downed a couple of glasses of wine to dispel her anxieties. Not any more. Not after losing her baby because of her drinking. Admittedly it had taken more than two glasses to relax her with all that had been going down at the time, but she felt sure the alcohol had cost her baby's life.

Don't go there. Not today. Please.

Her gaze followed the unfolding scenery. The farther from Nice central the more apartments came into view. Washing hung from balconies, bright flowering geraniums in pots decorated every available space. And between the buildings the bright blue of the sparkling Mediterranean. Then around a corner and houses clustered on the hillside, yellow and orange and red stone buildings tucked hard up against each other. Just like the pictures in the travel brochures, only more colourful, more vibrant and beautiful.

The next corner and the sea again, yachts of every size and shape bobbing gently in the current. A cruise ship took up a large portion of the picture, motorboats speeding to and from it.

Tori sat absorbing everything, letting her mind take a break, enjoying being in France. She snapped her camera far too many times, zooming in and out, sometimes finally getting the right frame only to have the train pass a power pole or tree as she pressed the button. The tension eased right back, her stomach stopped its ping-pong game, and she began to relax and put everything aside—for now.

At Ventimiglia, on the Italian border, she got off and went for a walk, had coffee and pizza and visited a market where she bought knick-knacks to take home. When she finally took the train back to Nice she was ready to face dinner with Ben and his friends.

'Where did you get to today?' Ben asked as they strolled through the old part of Nice to the restaurant Rita and John had chosen.

'Italy.' She smiled as three pairs of surprised eyes looked at her. 'I took the train along the coast, past Monaco, down to the border.'

'Had enough of the conference?' Rita asked, with a knowing glint in her look.

She winced. 'I know I shouldn't have gone away but, hey, when am I going to get back here again?' She wouldn't apologise, and she wouldn't allow that disappointed look in Ben's eyes to deflect her. This was her trip, and she had needed to step away from him. Anyway, she'd gone with Luc's blessing. What's more, it had worked. She was so much more relaxed and in control of her emotions since that train ride.

Rita shook her head. 'Fair enough. You obviously had a lovely time. You seem refreshed, if that's the word.'

John was watching her but didn't say anything. Thank goodness. Was he wondering if their conversation that morning had led to her taking the day off?

Time to change the subject. Tori tipped her head back to stare up at the building to their left. 'Aren't these amazing?' The stone walls were so old. History screamed at her. New Zealand was an *enfant* compared to Europe. At windows and narrow doors, meticulously worked wrought-iron balustrades made her mouth water. 'We've got nothing like this at home.'

Ben nodded. 'I like it that most buildings are not very high. The narrow streets don't feel closed in or as cool as they do in cities with high-rises.' He'd been a little cool himself since they'd met up in the hotel foyer half an hour ago. Probably having doubts about spending too much time with her.

'Here's the restaurant.' John indicated a group of tables and chairs ahead of them.

'Outdoor dining, perfect,' Tori said. 'Thanks for inviting me along.' This would be fun, and far better than eating on her own. As long as she kept relaxed and didn't let Ben dominate her mind.

Rita hugged her. 'You're welcome. Now, let's have fun.'

With great company and food, how could they not? As Tori sat on the chair Ben pulled out for her she sniffed the air. 'Garlic. Naturally.'

'Onions, seafood and oranges.' Ben nodded and seemed to be struggling not to smile. 'Are you ordering in French or English this time?'

'Definitely English. When I make up my mind what I'm eating I want to be sure I get it.' She turned to give him the once-over. 'You're as excited as I am.'

'You bet. Wait until we get to Paris.' His smile finally appeared.

Her stomach crunched. Paris. They weren't going together, but they would catch up at the medical school. Paris. Alone. Damn Ben. Why had he mentioned it? 'I'm looking forward to exploring the city.'

Ben tapped his fingers on her hand. 'Want to see the Eiffel Tower at night?' His gaze locked on hers.

'Of course.'

'With me?'

'Of course,' she answered before she could overthink his invitation. So much for remaining aloof, but Paris on her own wouldn't be half the fun as sharing the sights with Ben would be.

His smile widened. 'It's a date.'

A date? With her ex? As she sucked air into her lungs she met Rita's caring look and saw her nod. She'd already got the message that John thought she should be trying harder with Ben. Were they ganging up on her? Trying to undermine her determination to keep things between her and Ben ticking along in a friendly way— as in not in love? As her lungs pushed out air she said, 'It's a date.' The only one she'd have with Ben, but since she'd agreed, she was going to enjoy every minute of it, and to heck with her heart's relentless pounding.

She squashed down on the flicker of hope that there might be something in the future for her and Ben. She couldn't afford to hang her heart on that fragile wish. But...

What did I just do? Ben leaned back in his chair and stared at the menu in his hand. He didn't care what he ate any more. He shouldn't have invited Tori to go to the tower with him. How was that remaining remote and keeping his emotions in order?

Since her revelation about Dad that morning he'd been adamant he had to keep his distance. It wasn't what his father had suggested that got to him but that she'd believed in him, known he'd do what was right. It was what he'd expected, had barely hoped for on the bad days, but to have her tell him had shot straight at his heart, twisting the noose tighter. He was so screwed. He should've refused to come to Nice when he'd known Tori was going to be here.

But that had been impossible. Seven years of missing her, needing her—even when in denial—had driven him to take a risk. He had wanted so badly to see her again, had truly believed this would help him move on. And now he was making mistakes like saying they had a date.

'What are you ordering?' John asked from across the table.

The waiter was hovering at his elbow, ready to translate if needed.

Ben pointed to the menu. 'Steak, rare.'

Tori laughed and held her hand out to Rita. 'You owe me. Twenty euros, I believe.'

'What?' Ben looked from one smug woman to the other delving into her wallet to flourish a twenty-euro note.

'The girls had a bet on what you'd choose. Steak or seafood.'

And he'd missed that? Too much daydreaming and not enough concentration. Of course Tori would know what he'd choose. Steak had always been his favourite protein. 'We are in France. Obviously I'm eating steak.'

He tipped a nod at Tori. 'You're having paella.' She ate seafood in any way, shape or form at every opportunity.

Her smile melted his gloomy mood and put him back in his happy shoes. 'Duck *à l'orange*, or however it's said in French.'

So he'd got that wrong. He liked it that Tori could still surprise him. *I'm not meant to be liking anything about her too much.* True, but he was going to enjoy the evening anyway.

John ordered champagne, and sparkling water for Tori. 'You don't know what you're missing out on,' he told her.

'Sure I do.' Her smile dipped.

'When did you stop drinking wine?' Ben asked.

'A while back.'

'I remember…' He hesitated.

'That I drank too much.' A don't-go-there look had crept into her eyes. 'I'm sure you do.'

When you said to drink French champagne in France would be the ultimate dream. Looks like she'd got over that.

'Let's order,' Rita intervened, after a quick glance at Tori.

The food was delicious, made more so by the setting and the company. At last Ben pushed his dessert plate aside and reached for his wine glass. He hadn't had such a wonderful night in a long while. 'Thanks, everyone. A great evening.' He raised his glass to his friends. Tori? A friend? For lack of a better word, yes, but it didn't sit easily. She was more than a friend, less than his wife.

'I agree.' John tapped his nearly full glass against everyone else's and put it down, the wine untouched.

'John? Something wrong with your wine?' The man

was a wine connoisseur, never missed an opportunity to try new vintages.

He gave a single shake of his head. 'It's fine.'

It should be, given it was one of the biggest names for red wine on the continent. About to push John about it, Ben backed off. If his mate didn't want to say anything, then he'd respect that. He mightn't want to be heard criticising the wine in front of the waiters.

Rita said, 'You don't want your dessert, either? Can I try some?'

'Go ahead.' John pushed his plate towards his wife. 'I knew you wouldn't be able to resist.'

'It's chocolate. Of course I have to have some.' Rita spooned up a small mouthful.

John said, 'I think I'm having a heart attack.'

What? Cold dread filled Ben. 'John? Tori, get an ambulance.' He was on his feet and at John's side in an instant. 'I'm taking your pulse, man. You're sweating. Where exactly is this pain?'

'Onto it.' Tori was already halfway across the dining area, hurrying towards the head waiter. She was waving her hands and pointing to their table as she talked rapidly. Hopefully the waiter understood enough English to get the gist of her request. Now was not the time to have to be trying out her schoolgirl French.

Rita's spoon clattered onto her plate. 'John? Please, tell me this is a joke.'

John lifted his hand to his chest, rubbed round and round over his ribs, his heart, even up to his shoulder. 'Here.'

Rita cried, 'John? Hold on for that ambulance. Think of the kids. Please.' Her hand gripped John's. 'Don't you dare go getting sick, love. You can't.' Despair had crept into her voice.

Ben touched her shoulder. 'We'll soon have John in hospital.' He had no idea what the response time would be like here, or how far away the hospital was.

'There's a hotel full of cardiologists ten minutes away,' John quipped around a pain-filled grimace. 'I'll be fine, sweetheart.'

Oh, sure. Ben barely stopped himself rolling his eyes. John was only trying to cheer up Rita, but one quick look at her told him how much she believed that.

'They're phoning for the ambulance now.' Tori was back.

'How can you be sure what they're doing?' The wobble in Rita's voice was awful.

Tori wrapped an arm around Rita's waist. 'I talked to a patron who spoke English and French. She's organising everything.'

John groaned and pitched forward into Ben's arms.

'Steady, mate. Let's get you lying down.'

A woman appeared by their table. 'There's a sofa inside that the waiter says you can use for your friend.'

'Thank you,' Tori answered. 'Now we need a man to help Ben shift John in there.'

'The waiter's willing to help.' The woman fired off what was required to the man at her elbow.

Ben stood up with John draped over him. 'Come on, mate. We're taking you in where you'll be more comfortable.'

John wasn't answering. His mouth was slack and drooling.

'Quickly, help me.' Ben swallowed down on the flare of panic. This was not happening to John. No way in hell.

Even as the woman translated the waiter was taking

John's other side. Between them they shuffled John inside and laid him on the sofa.

Tori brought Rita inside and gently pressed her onto a chair. 'I'm going to help Ben, okay? John's in good hands.'

Ben was counting John's respiratory rate as he undid his tie and tore open his shirt. 'How's that pain, John?'

'Worse,' John croaked, then screwed his eyes tight.

'I'm taking your pulse,' Tori told him, her eyes scanning John's face. 'Very pale,' she murmured.

'Have you had pain like this before?' Ben asked. Resp rate was low.

'No,' John muttered.

'Pulse faint.' Tori added to the dire picture.

The woman who'd called for the ambulance said, 'Do you want me to stay and interpret for you when the paramedics arrive?'

'Yes, please. You can start by telling them we're both cardiac specialists.' They'd understand everything possible had been done correctly.

John's head lolled to one side.

Tori flicked her head up. 'Pulse gone.'

Rita cried out. The woman moved to her side.

Ben stood and pulled John onto the floor so there was something hard under his body. 'Tori, I'll take the compressions, you do the breaths.'

'Onto it.' She knelt at John's head, snatched a cushion from a chair and gently slid it under John, tipping his head back to clear the throat.

Ben's laced hands were already regularly pressing down hard on John's sternum. 'Five, six, seven.' *Where the hell's that ambulance?*

Tori looked around, back to him and shook her head once.

Had he spoken aloud? Or had she read his mind? He hoped the second option as he didn't want to terrify Rita any more than she already was. But that ambulance was needed right now. If not minutes ago. There'd be a defibrillator on board to shock John. Hopefully bring him back to life. How far away was the nearest hospital? Or the ambulance station—if they had that system here. Why in France, John? *I feel hog-tied.* The language is foreign, the system unknown. But it didn't really matter where they were. This was John, his best mate, and at the moment he'd give anything to see him open his eyes and ask what was going on.

'Twenty-one, twenty-two.'

Tori was ready to breathe two lungfuls of air into John the moment Ben reached thirty compressions. Then they'd start all over again. And again. Damn, he had never felt so helpless.

His shoulders were tight, his arms already feeling a pain, but he'd keep going for as long as it took. This was John.

The sound of a siren filled him with relief but he didn't stop the compressions until two paramedics carrying a medical kit and the most important defibrillator he'd ever set his gaze on were beside him and calmly, quickly going about their jobs, attaching the pads for the electric current to John's chest, feeling the carotid to confirm what was obvious but had to be checked.

An ECG machine was applied as well, the flat line terrifying, despite how often Ben had witnessed that in his career. He looked for the woman to translate. 'Tell them he went into cardiac arrest less than three minutes ago.' Still time to get a favourable outcome. Barely, but barely was better than not at all.

As the paramedics took over, Ben stepped back,

reluctant to let go but aware these men knew how to do their jobs as well as he did. He reached for Rita, wrapped her in a hug. There was nothing he could say to alleviate her fear so he kept quiet. On his other side Tori stood watching every action, her body tight with worry.

When one of the paramedics called out something they stepped back, before the woman had even interpreted the phrase as stand clear. They all stared at the monitor reading John's heart, willing him back to life. Nothing happened.

'Come on, John,' Rita cried. 'You can do it. You have to. Damn you, start breathing.' Tears streamed down her cheeks. 'John. Please. Remember the kids.'

Her anguish cut Ben deep. He felt so useless. A cardiac specialist and right now there was nothing he could do to save his friend's life. He felt a hand on his arm, knew it was Tori. Thank goodness she was here with them. Her presence couldn't change the outcome, but he did feel something soft curl around his heart because of her. She was rooting for John and Rita, for him. And right now he needed her.

If the worst happened… He gagged. *It won't. It can't.*

'Stand clear.' The paramedic had reset the defibrillator.

John's body partially lifted off the floor. Then he slammed back down, his head hitting the cushion.

'We've got a pulse.' At least Ben presumed that's what the grimly smiling paramedic said to them as he pointed to the ECG machine.

Ben watched that line on the tiny screen as it flicked up and down, no longer ruler straight at the bottom of the picture. John wasn't out of trouble yet, but he was a damned sight better off than he had been seconds ago.

Rita collapsed against him, her body racked with shivers. 'Is he...? Will he...?'

'Shh. At the moment John's heart is working, though nowhere near perfectly.' That was going to take diagnosis and treatment, and a lot of time in bed. If he was lucky. 'He's breathing again.' He'd learned at the beginning of his career to keep things simple when patients' relatives were in shock. Rita was no slug but right now she'd barely be absorbing any details except that John was alive. 'These men will transfer him to hospital where he'll be put onto a heart support machine to be monitored thoroughly.'

One of the paramedics held up a plastic board with a sheet clipped to it. *'Nom?'*

'He needs John's details,' Tori said as she took the board. 'What's John's full name, Rita?'

'John Barry McIntyre.'

'Date of birth?'

Surprisingly quickly, Tori had filled in every line and was handing back the information. When the paramedic asked her another question she tipped her head slightly. 'Pardon?'

The helpful woman stepped up. 'He's telling you to bring insurance details to the hospital.'

'But that's back in our hotel. I'm not going there. I'm going with John.' Rita turned to look at her husband. 'I'm not letting him out of my sight.'

Tori took her hand. 'Tell me where you keep your travel documents and I'll go get them. Though if you've got your credit card with you, that's probably all you need to get sorted.'

'Will you? Everything's in the safe, and our code is four-five-three-two.'

'I'll need your room key.' Tori spoke softly.

'*Duh*. Of course. Tori, will John be all right now?'

Ben's stomach clenched at the unfair but expected question. No one knew the answer to that. He saved Tori by saying, 'Rita, John is gravely ill. But he is alive. Hang on to that.'

Rita's bottom lip trembled. 'I understand. I was looking for rainbows.'

Tori gave her a sad smile. 'I like that. Rainbows. You hang on to yours. Now, where's our new friend? We need taxis and to find out where they're taking John.'

'All sorted,' she was told. 'One taxi will go to the hospital and the other will take you to the hotel and wait to take you to the hospital when you're ready.'

Ben reached out and shook her hand. 'Thank you for everything.'

'You're welcome. I hope all goes well for you.' She nodded to Rita. 'Times like this you wish you were at home, I know.'

Never a truer word, Ben thought as he led Rita out to their taxi. But at least they could be thankful for the excellent hospitals here. Watching John being loaded into the ambulance, he said, 'Rita, you can go with John.'

'I'd like to. Would they mind?'

'Looks to me like they're waving you over. Go on. I'll be right behind you all the way.' If John arrested again the ambulance would pull over while the paramedics tried to resuscitate him and he'd be in that ambulance fast. But it wouldn't be easy for Rita, being stuck in there and not understanding a word the men might say. Still he added, 'You'll be fine.'

As the back doors closed John and Rita in, Ben looked around for Tori. 'Hey,' he called as she was about to get into her taxi.

'Hey, yourself.' Her smile was tired but full of

understanding and something else. Not love? No, he'd got that wrong. Just because he wanted it, it didn't mean he was going to get it. 'See you shortly.'

Then she was gone, the taxi speeding down the narrow road as though John was the passenger and not Tori.

Tori. There when he'd needed her. Quietly efficient, backing his every move, even being one step ahead of him at times. Tori. They'd been in sync—unlike the end days of their marriage.

The taxi moved forwards, tailing the ambulance, his driver obviously not finding it necessary to get him to the hospital any sooner than John. Which suited Ben just fine. He wanted to know if John had another heart failure. Wanted to be there for him, and Rita.

God damn, John. How long have you been feeling unwell? All day? All week? Longer?

Ben thought back to the first moment he'd seen his friend on day one of the conference. Other than the weight gain John had looked fine. But he'd been quiet throughout dinner, hardly touching his food. *Well, mate, you're going to get a telling off for scaring Rita and me. And Tori.*

Tori. Her name spun into his mind so fast he gasped. His wife. Ex maybe, but still Tori. Not quite as he remembered her. She didn't laugh so much these days, hardly at all really, and one of the things he'd loved about her was her laughter. Everything and anything had brought that deep, heart-warming sound bubbling over her lips. She'd taken her career seriously but she'd been full of sunshine and happiness.

'Ici, monsieur.'

'What?' Ben looked around, surprised to find they were at the hospital and the ambulance was backing into the emergency bay. He handed over far too much money

and leapt out to go be with Rita. He had her and John
to think about now. Nothing else mattered until John's
prognosis was good and he was on the road to recovery.

Nothing else.

No one else.

How long will it take you to get here, Tori?

CHAPTER SIX

'GO AND GET something to eat, you two.' Rita stood before them, looking exhausted and somehow smaller. 'Or have a strong coffee anyway.'

Tori eased herself up from the uncomfortable, moulded plastic chair she'd spent half the night on, and stretched up onto her toes, bent backwards to undo some of the kinks in her muscles. It had been a long night sitting outside the intensive care unit, gleaning the occasional piece of information about John's progress. 'Not hungry, but I could murder a coffee. Why don't you come with us? We can go to the hospital cafeteria so you're not far away from John.'

Ben slowly unwound his tall frame and came to his feet. 'How's he doing now?'

Rita dragged her hands down her pale cheeks. 'Holding his own. The doctor says he needs complete rest and quiet. He's been very lucky. We've been extraordinarily lucky.'

This lovely couple had had a second chance. They *were* lucky. In some ways Tori hoped Rita didn't understand how close she'd come to losing her husband or she'd spend the rest of her life worrying about him every time he so much as winced. During the night Monsieur Leclare had come to the hospital after hearing about

John's heart attack from the specialist treating him. The fact they were all attending the conference had made short work of the barriers usually surrounding a patient. Rita had been adamant that Tori and Ben be in on any conversation about John's condition, and Luc had been exemplary in explaining everything.

Tori repeated, 'Come with us for a short break.'

Rita shook her head. 'No. The nurses have been wonderful with a continuous supply of coffee and anything else I want. You both need to get some fresh air, and…' She held up her hand, palm out. 'Before you even think it, I don't need one of you staying here while the other takes a break. Go somewhere decent, take your time. Have a shower back at the hotel. Grab a couple of hours' sleep.' Was that a wicked glint in her eye? Couldn't be. Not after the night she'd just endured. But she certainly sounded far more confident this morning. Guess John's improving condition would do that. 'Then, Tori, can you please bring me a change of clothes so I can make the most of the bathroom facilities here.'

Tori hugged her. 'You sure know how to twist my arm. We'll go but only if you promise to phone if anything changes.'

'Anything at all,' Ben underlined her comment. Then dropped a chaste kiss on Rita's brow.

'Promise.'

Outside Tori shivered and rubbed her hands up and down her arms. The sky was overcast for the first time since she'd arrived in Nice. As though the weather had come out in sympathy with Rita and John. *Rita and that look.* It was almost as if she was playing at matchmaking. Sometime when Rita was less preoccupied, she'd have to explain to her that she and Ben getting back together was impossible.

Why? Because—just because.

But Ben didn't seem to be having any hesitation about them getting along together. He said, 'Come here.'

When he tucked her in against his body she didn't resist, pushed all her doubts aside for a while. His strength helped her walk across the road. Until now she hadn't realised how exhausted she was. It was nearly eight o'clock. 'That was a long night.'

'Interminable. We should be used to it, but somehow this was different.'

'Personal.' And she'd only met this couple three days ago. They were Ben's best friends. 'Are you okay?'

'I don't mind admitting this has rocked me. John's only a couple of years older than me. Yes, I know that means zero in the scheme of things and that hearts will do what they do regardless of what we mortals think is normal, but this time it's different. Frightening, to be truthful. He hasn't been unwell.' Ben paused on the edge of the pavement. 'Want to go back to the hotel for breakfast and that shower?'

'I don't fancy being questioned by people interested in knowing how John is, however well meaning they are.' She presumed word had got around. Working in hospitals had taught her there was no such thing as a secret amongst medical personnel. Discretion, yes, sometimes; out and out keeping quiet, no. A yawn ripped through her. 'Let's see if there's a decent café close by.'

Ben waved down a taxi. 'I've a better idea. We'll order room service at the hotel. It does mean running the gauntlet in Reception but hopefully most people will be at breakfast, or they're taking a leisurely start to the day since the conference is over.'

Suddenly Ben's idea seemed the best thing she'd heard in ages. 'Let's go.'

She barely noticed the ride down to the hotel or the ride up in the lift. But even through the fog of exhaustion she was aware of Ben at her side, of him following her into her room.

'How long?' Tori asked, as Ben put the phone down from ordering full English breakfasts for them both. Tori was thankful they'd come to her room because it meant she didn't have far to go to crawl into the shower and ease the aches in her body as soon as they'd eaten.

Ben ran a hand down his face. 'Twenty minutes max. I hope I can stay awake that long.'

'So do I.' Ben falling asleep in her room wasn't an option.

Ben paced to the window and jammed his hands on his hips. 'I could kill John for frightening us like that.'

Tori found the energy to get up and cross to him. Winding her arms around his waist, she laid her head on his chest. 'You okay?'

'I guess.' Ben's hands spread across her back, holding her gently against him.

They stood there saying nothing more, holding each other, taking and giving comfort. Tori didn't mind if breakfast never arrived. This was way more energising—as long as she didn't have to move.

But eventually there was a loud rapping on the door. 'Room service.'

Ben placed a light kiss on her brow before going to let the waiter in. As the aroma of hot bacon tickled her senses Tori had to admit she might've been premature in thinking she could forgo eating. But it was one heck of a toss-up—being in Ben's arms or breakfast. Her finger traced where his lips had touched her. Yes, she could forgo eating to spend time kissing Benji, but that would be the most unwise thing she could ever do.

'What's making you smile like that?' the man who'd left his kiss on her brow asked, after seeing the waiter out with a hefty tip.

Tori shook her head. 'Probably exhaustion.'

'I know what you mean.' Ben's gaze strayed in the direction of the big bed dominating the room. 'I'm worried if I lie down for those couple of hours Rita suggested I might not wake up until nighttime.'

We're not sharing a bed so that we can wake each other. Even in this state we wouldn't go to sleep. 'Both of us need to catch some shut-eye. I'm going to set the alarm on my phone *and* ask Reception to call me at ten-thirty.'

That wasn't disappointment in Ben's eyes. Was it? He turned slowly to the small table and sank onto a chair. 'Let's eat.'

The food perked up Tori's spirits. 'Think I'll go and get Rita's clothes in case we have to head back to the hospital in a hurry.'

Ben nodded. 'Okay with you if I have another coffee? I'll be gone in a few minutes.'

'Take your time. I won't be long. Rita and John's room is only one floor up.'

'If it's rush hour in Reception, with people checking out, it could take for ever to get an elevator.' Ben yawned and rubbed his hand over his stubbly chin.

Tori turned for the door before the urge to run her hand over those sexy angles got the better of her. 'Meet you downstairs at eleven, unless anything changes.'

Ten minutes later she was back in her room and staring at the man sprawled across her bed—sound asleep. 'So you do still take up all the space.'

Ben must've collapsed onto the bed in a daze. He hadn't even removed his shoes. Tori carefully undid the laces and pulled the shoes off. Then she slipped out of her own, tugged her dress over her head and slid under the covers, squeezing into what little space wasn't held down by some part of her husband. Ex-husband. Benji or Ben. Didn't matter which. He was the only man she'd ever loved so completely, but he was an ex. Unfortunately. *Shut up, Tori.*

A soft snore broke the silence and she smiled. She remembered those, too. *It's a snore, for pity's sake.* Her eyelids slowly closed, her breathing deepened as she listened for Ben's next sound. It was warm in here, and awkward when she tried to move her legs because there was nowhere to put them in the small space left by Ben. Citrusy pine scent relaxed her further, so that her body softened into the mattress. Carefully rolling onto her side, she curled up and gave in to the sleep tugging at her.

The alarm was harsh, the bleating phone worse. Tori blinked awake and reached first for the hotel phone. There was a weight around her waist. Warm and heavy, and comfortable. Familiar.

'*Merci,*' she muttered into the phone and hung up, slid her mobile phone alarm to Off.

'That went too fast,' Ben growled in her ear.

Rolling over, Tori came face-to-face with him, and this time she did run her fingertips over his stubble-darkened chin. 'You were asleep when I got back from Rita's room.'

'I was drinking coffee. How did I end up on your bed?' he whispered. Then, 'Who cares how? I'm here and I slept.' His eyes held the rest of that sentence. *With you.*

Sort of with her. Ben still lay on the outside while the bedcover hid her body from sight. Her dressed-only-in-lingerie body. 'You're going to have to leave so I can get up.'

'In a moment.' His head was inches from hers. Those startling eyes watched her with an intensity that reached deep inside her. That mouth that could do the most amazing things on her skin looked soft after sleep. His arm was still on her waist, only now she was being pulled closer to his body. 'I've missed you, Tori. I've missed us.'

'We were great together.' What was she talking about? Their lovemaking? Or everything? Their life, their love, everything.

'Did we give up too easily?' he whispered, just before his lips brushed her forehead, then trailed down her cheek to her mouth.

'Ben,' she cried softly against his mouth, and her lips opened, pressed against his. *Ben. Benji.* Her heart.

Their mouths became one, moulded together, while their tongues got reacquainted.

I remember this.

Ben pulled her closer still so there was only the bedcover between them. All the while they kissed. Her eyes were wide open, watching him, drinking in every line, each eyebrow hair, his eyes that were watching her back. Benji.

This was us.

Kissing Benji had always been her favourite way to start the day. His passion and love set her up and made her feel good. Like she was beginning to feel now. Warmth stole from their joined mouths, moved down to her breasts and the peaks that were tightening. Down to her stomach and beyond to that place that needed Ben, had missed him for so long, was moistening in readiness for him. Could they find the way back to each other? Right now anything seemed possible.

'Hell.' Ben pulled away and flopped onto his back. 'Sorry.'

Talk about poking a needle into a balloon. Tori sat up. 'You're sorry?' That was about as insulting as it could get. The fact that they shouldn't have been kissing had nothing to do with anything. Worse, she wanted him so badly her body ached with need. All because of one kiss. A passionate kiss filled with memories and all the things she'd missed for so long.

Ben got off the bed, picked up his shoes. Turned to lock his eyes on her. 'Yes, I am because I know it's not what you want—despite your ardent reaction.'

Heat coloured her cheeks. She'd been that obvious, huh? Of course she had. 'It's not what you want, either, Ben.' *It's over. We don't belong together.* The words she'd never forgotten had finally found the right moment to remind her of the truth. Ben had left her, and had gone as far away as he could possibly get. They weren't getting back together so that meant they weren't even having a brief interlude filled with kisses—or sex. But a girl could hope for different.

He sat on a chair and shoved his feet into his shoes. As he knotted the laces he growled, 'I've been wanting to kiss you from the moment I said hello on the first morning of the conference.'

And now that you have? Her mouth opened but there were no words to combat this startling revelation. He couldn't have wanted that. Not after all this time. *But you came awake to him in an instant. Why shouldn't Ben be the same?*

'One kiss wasn't enough, Tori.' Standing up, he headed for the door. 'Meet you in the lobby in half an hour.'

The door clicked shut behind him. Tori stared around the room. Had Ben really been here? Or had she dreamt everything? That would be worse, dreaming he might want her. That would show her own fantasies were way off track. They weren't meant to get back together. One sniff of the pillow he'd used and she had all the proof she needed. Burying her face in the softness that held his particular scent, she gave in to the longing that had gripped her from the moment she'd first heard him say her name four days ago.

Ben hadn't said anything about getting back together. He'd only wanted to kiss her. Relationships were more than a kiss. Or multiple kisses.

Her fingers covered her lips as she stumbled into the bathroom. But kisses were how relationships started. Yeah, and they finished with harsh, hurtful words. Words she'd better remember.

Ben was still berating himself over kissing Tori when they got out of the taxi outside the hospital. How could he have done that? How could he have been foolish enough to say it hadn't been enough?

Because when she'd blinked at him with those sleep-filled eyes there was nothing on this planet that could've stopped him. The need to kiss her had been steadily building up all the time they'd been here. Add in the stress of John's sudden near-death and he'd been a lost cause. Waking up in her room, on her bed, with her right beside him, had thrown him, addling his usually sharp brain.

But that kiss... His heart squeezed. Tori. It had taken years to get some semblance of normality in his life, and now he'd be starting over.

Reaching for Rita's bag at the same time as Tori,

their fingers touched and Tori withdrew fast. 'I'll take that,' he muttered.

'Fine.' Her shoulders were taut as she led the way inside to the elevators.

He wasn't going to let her keep this up. She'd been as much a part of that kiss as he had. Sure, he'd started it, but not once had she hesitated. He'd have stopped if she had. They were adults, they could get past this and be friends again. As much as they'd been friends before. 'When are you planning on heading to Paris?'

Tori's shoulders lifted on a sigh. 'Tomorrow.'

Not good enough, Tori. 'Flying?'

'Train.'

'So what were your plans for today? Before John's heart attack happened?'

She stepped into the elevator and turned to him. Tears glittered on her eyelashes. 'I had a sightseeing trip booked.' Her hand dashed across her eyes. 'But that's the last thing I feel like doing now. I'll sit with Rita, or with John while she has a sleep if that's what she wants.'

You and me both. But why the tears? 'Good luck with that. Rita will have her own agenda.' Like coming up with suggestions about how he and Tori should spend their day together. He'd have to tell Rita to back off on that one, that he'd sort out his relationship himself.

Tori shook her head and that glorious hair swirled over her back. 'She's tough, isn't she?' Blink, blink.

'Why are you crying? Or trying desperately not to?' He hated it when she cried, felt her pain and wanted to banish it. He'd always felt as though he was to blame, that he should've kept her so happy there'd be no need for tears.

Her eyes met his. 'You know what? I'm not entirely

sure. These past fourteen hours have been a bit of an emotional roller coaster.'

That included their kiss, right? 'I agree.'

'Ben, I don't understand what's going on.'

He knew she had to be talking about them. It was there in her face, in the pain and confusion. He'd seen that in those very eyes before. On the day he'd told her he was leaving. The day he'd readily expunge from their lives if there was a chance to rewrite their history.

The elevator glided to a stop and the door slid open. Taking Tori's elbow, he led her out and along the wide corridor to Intensive Care. Just before they reached the nurses' station to check if it was okay to visit, he told Tori, 'I'm not sure I understand everything, either, but I'd like the opportunity to find out.' His bottom lip was unsteady when he drew a breath. 'Would you spend some time with me in Paris, Tori? See if we can't come up an answer?'

The breath he'd drawn stuck in his lungs, making the intercostal muscles hurt as he waited, and waited. Her eyes had widened with surprise—or shock. But she hadn't run away like he was a madman.

Finally, just when he thought he'd need medical intervention to start breathing again, she said so quietly he hoped he heard correctly, 'I'd like that.'

'Good. Great.' The air whooshed over his lips that were already curving up into a smile. He had to haul the brakes on that smile in case he came across as too keen. But he was eager to get started on this journey with Tori, to see where it led them. Back to what they'd once had seemed too much to hope for; anything less seemed too horrible to contemplate. Tori. His wife. He didn't think of her as his ex. That seemed too impersonal, or full of angry emotions that weren't there in their case, or wrong. Yes, definitely wrong. 'Where do we start?' he muttered, more to himself than her.

'Let's go and see John.' Tori was being ever practical. 'We might be staying in Nice for a few days yet.'

A nurse went to inform Rita that they were back and returned to say they could both go in as Rita would like to have a shower and try to sleep a bit.

Rita hugged them both. Her eyes were red and puffy. 'The doctors have been around. Monsieur Leclare came with them and interpreted everything for us. John's scheduled to have two angioplasty stents inserted in his artery tomorrow.' Fear filled her weary eyes. 'He will be all right, won't he?' She stared from him to Tori and back to him.

Ben slipped an arm around her shoulders. 'That's standard procedure for blocked arteries.'

John muttered from the bed, 'I'll be up and about sooner than you can believe.'

Ben nodded and asked Rita, 'Did Luc explain to you how the stent's put in?'

'You mean about putting the wire into his artery at the groin and pushing the stent up to the blockage? Yes. That's spooky, but if it's what's done then let's get it over with as soon as possible.' Rita took the tissues Tori was handing her and glared down at her husband. 'Hopefully then you won't have another heart attack.'

'You're going to have to change his diet.' Ben couldn't help himself, even when he knew both John and Rita would be fully aware of that. It was just too important to ignore.

'Give me the easy job, why don't you?' A slight smile hovered on Rita's lips.

Tori did better with her smile. 'You like your food, then, John?'

Rita didn't give him a chance to answer. 'Oh, yes. You'd think with his job he'd live on lettuce but, no, not a chance. Until now. He is going to be living so healthily it will be embarrassing.' Tears slid down her face. 'Everyone's been absolutely wonderful, but I just want to go home, take John back to where everything's familiar.'

Tori nodded. 'Unfortunately he should probably rest a few days at least before making that long haul back to Sydney.'

Ben had the answer. 'As soon as the doctors say John can move, you're going to London and my apartment. You'll be comfortable there, and there'll be less stress with no language issues.'

'Phew, that's a load off my mind.' Rita looked infinitesimally happier. 'Can I bring the kids over to join us? They won't be a problem in the apartment, I promise.'

'Those scallywags will have a blast. I'll book the flights later today.'

John raised a thumb. 'Good.'

'You'll have to go by train to London. There's no flying for John for a little while.'

Again John nodded, but, then, he'd already know that. 'Rita.' He spoke softly. 'She needs a break.'

'On her way. You're going to have to put up with Tori and me for the next few hours. We're the official babysitters.' Ben pulled a chair up to the bed and sat down to prove he wasn't going anywhere. 'Want me to read you a bedtime story?'

'The only ones I can think of aren't appropriate in the current company.' John gave him a feeble smile.

'Go to sleep, buddy. You need it.'

'You don't need to hang around, watching over me. There are more than enough nurses doing that already.'

John's voice faded in and out, like he was half-asleep already.

'That's why I'm staying. To share the nurses,' he quipped, his gaze already drifting across to Tori, who was talking with Rita. There wasn't a nurse in the hospital, or any other woman anywhere, who could snag his attention. There was only one woman he was interested in, had ever been in love with, and she was only a few feet away. Might as well be on the other side of the world for all the good that was doing him.

But Tori had agreed to spend time with him, to see how they got on.

'She's the one, isn't she?'

And he'd thought John was falling asleep. 'The only one,' he admitted quietly.

Just admitting it to his friend showed how out of control his emotions had become. Tori did that to him. Had done it right from that first glimpse of her in the department all those years back. From that moment he'd been hooked. Nothing that had happened later on had changed a thing. He'd never stopped loving her, no matter how hard he'd tried. He'd been fooling himself all along so that life was easier to cope with. Sure, he'd thought he'd made progress, could go along for months without thinking about her, then she'd be there in the front of his mind, beckoning, refusing to go away. Despite what he'd told her, he'd never fallen out of love with her.

He hadn't trusted her love as much as he should've, but he'd always believed he'd been doing the right thing by Tori when he'd left her.

He shoved the fingers of one hand through his hair. 'Was I right? Or was I wrong?' he whispered to himself.

'I don't know the details, but from what I've seen these past few days I'm thinking wrong.'

No problem with John's hearing, then. 'You and me both.'

Tori was hugging Rita. They'd bonded so quickly and easily. Tori had always had a big heart, and yet she'd never had many close friends. Just Diane and Lynley, the two girls she'd grown up with.

I want her back. So I can't stuff it up this time. Slowly, slowly.

'You've got a few days so make them count.'

'John, you're meant to be going to sleep, not sorting out my life.'

'I've just learned how quickly life can change. Don't let Tori get away—not without giving your absolute best shot.'

Ben swallowed hard. So said the man who'd nearly left them for ever last night. What would he have done if John had died? He'd have been beyond devastated. Just as he'd been when he'd pushed Tori out of his life. 'I'll make you a deal, buddy. You get some sleep and I'll start with being up-front with Tori about a few things.' When she got back from accompanying Rita to the room the hospital staff had found for her.

The gleam in John's eyes almost made Ben feel guilty for not mentioning he'd already made a move with Tori, that he'd kissed her and they'd agreed to spend time together. But even as his best friend, John wasn't going to be privy to everything going on in his head—make that in his heart. Not when getting closer to Tori was still most likely to turn belly-up. How could they have a relationship when living at opposite ends of the world? He felt John's hand on his.

Then his buddy was saying, 'I haven't said it yet, but thank you. I wouldn't be...' John couldn't get the rest of his sentence out.

'Don't go there. Anyway, Tori had as much input.' They'd worked together, each doing their job without hesitation. The only focus had been to save John, and they'd succeeded.

He and Tori working together. Surely that had to be a sign. A good one.

CHAPTER SEVEN

'THIS IS LA DAME DE LA COEUR,' Marc Dupont told a tiny girl made to look even smaller by the big bed she lay in.

Marc had heard about her talk at the conference, and after checking John's obs had invited Tori to visit the children's ward with him. Since she'd canned the idea of sightseeing, she was happy to oblige.

'Maelee, say hello to the doctor.'

The pale child glanced back and forth between Tori and her specialist. Her laboured breathing spoke of heart disease. *'Bonjour,'* she finally wheezed.

'Bonjour, Maelee.' Tori shifted closer to the bed and crouched down so she wasn't towering over the girl. 'I am from another country far away, New Zealand.'

From Maelee's bewildered expression her pronunciation wasn't even close.

Tori tried again. 'I look after sick girls and boys back at my home.'

Thankfully Marc interpreted her diabolical accent and Maelee's eyes lit up. 'You want to see me?'

With Marc's help Tori chatted to the little girl and gained her confidence. 'How old are you, Maelee?'

'Six.'

Six. Too young to be dealing with this. 'What do you like doing when you're at home?' What would her child have liked to do at this age? She or he would've been six now, too. *Would they have pestered me for a horse, like I did my mum?*

'Computer games.' She paused to get her breathing under control. 'But I want to ride my bike, like my friends can.'

You poor wee pet. Pulling out her phone, Tori showed Maelee a picture of Dean Cox. 'This boy has a sore heart, too.'

'But he's laughing and waving.'

'That's because we've made him better. He was going home when that photo was taken.'

Maelee stared at Dean. 'I like him. I want to go home.'

Tori knew the child was having surgery for a faulty aortic valve in the morning. 'You need to get better first. That's what Dean had to do.' Then she asked, 'Can I listen to your heart, Maelee?'

'Oui.' Maelee instantly hauled up her pyjama top and exposed her skinny chest. 'It's going bang-bang-bang.'

Taking the stethoscope Marc handed her, Tori listened to the erratic beating of the girl's heart. Meeting the specialist's eyes, she nodded. This was a very sick child, and after surgery tomorrow she'd be spending the next few days in the intensive care unit where John was currently laid up.

Gently pulling Maelee's top down, Tori asked, 'Can I tell Dean about you? I'm sure he'd like to send you a message.'

Maelee nodded, and Tori typed a quick message to Dean about the little French girl.

The brief message had hardly gone and Dean was answering.

Hi, Heart Lady. Why are you in a hospital? Aren't you coming home?

He should be sound asleep at this hour. Dean's mother would be growling at her for disturbing her son. It would be after midnight back in New Zealand. Her smile turned to worry. Was Dean having sleep issues again? Before she'd operated he'd always been exhausted and yet unable to sleep well. She replied.

Of course I'm coming home. I want to see you again. Do you have a message for Maelee?

Tell her to be brave and that she's going to get better soon, like me.

After passing on Dean's message, Tori followed Marc out of the ward to discuss tomorrow's surgery. 'Why did it take so long for Maelee to get specialist treatment?'

'Her mother ignored the signs, and it wasn't until Maelee became ill at school one day that the nurse picked up on her breathing and heart rhythm. The faulty valve is congenital due to the mother having had rubella during her pregnancy.'

'The mother didn't follow up on getting her baby checked after birth?'

Marc shook his head. 'She says she did, but Maelee's symptoms didn't present until she was nearly five.'

The child should've been monitored right from birth, but not knowing the full details of the case Tori didn't say a word. Anyway, it was more likely the mother hadn't been vigilant than the health system failing Maelee. 'I'll see her when I visit John in the afternoon,' Tori told Marc. 'If you're happy with that,' she added hurriedly.

'Very happy. *Merci.*'

Tori headed back to Intensive Care, but before going in she sent an email to her clinic head nurse.

I'm concerned about Dean. Seems he might not be sleeping properly. I'd like you to arrange for him to come in for a check-up with Conrad ASAP.

Conrad had joined her clinic six months ago for post-grad work and was talking about moving to England when the year was up. Tori didn't want him to go as he'd become such an asset to the clinic. His medical skills were invaluable and the children adored his jokes and games.

She sighed. Get over it. It wasn't as though she hadn't known he'd be moving on. But having to take on yet another new, and most likely temporary, doctor always had everyone on edge for the first few days. In some cases, first few weeks. Not that she could fault Conrad's thinking. He wanted to get as much experience under his belt as possible before settling into a full-time practice. Another sigh trickled over her lips.

'What's with all the sighing?' Ben asked from behind her.

Tori almost leapt off the floor, she'd been so engrossed in her thoughts about home. Home—the clinic really was her home. She mightn't have a bed of her own or a wardrobe there, but she spent most hours of the day and night in the place. *Just like old times.* She hadn't cut back on those hideous hours at all, instead using them to hide from reality. Shock rippled through her. She didn't have a life outside work.

'Tori, have I grown a wart on my nose?' Ben chided.

Shaking away the revelation that had slammed into

her, she said, 'Just keeping tabs on a patient back home.'
She explained to Ben about the email and Dean, ignoring the bouncing exclamation in her head... *You don't have a life other than as a cardiologist. You don't have a life other than as a cardiologist.* What had she been saying? Patient. Dean. Tori then mentioned Conrad. 'He's too good to let go, but I can't find the incentive needed to keep him with us permanently.'

'It's not unusual for newly qualified residents to head overseas for work experience,' Ben agreed. 'Have you thought of offering him a place for when he returns?'

'Tried that, thinking I could lock him into one year away, but he's reluctant to tie himself down. I'm being silly. It's not like I have trouble getting doctors to work with us.'

'But you hate change.' Ben grinned.

Laughter bubbled up, banishing her despondency. 'You haven't forgotten anything, have you?'

His grin widened as he rolled his eyes. 'Why can't we go to the movies on Sunday afternoon, Tori?' Then he mimicked her. 'I like going on Saturdays, that's why. It's what I'm used to.'

She flicked his arm with the back of her hand. 'I never.'

'Oh, really?'

'Okay, maybe I did like routine, but movies only on Saturdays? I don't think so.'

'In the interests of not having an argument I will resist the temptation to remind you of other similar...' he flicked fingers in the air '...routines we lived by and instead will invite you to join me for a walk through the old city area. I hear there's lots of wonderful art and antiques there.'

'You got me.' Then she hesitated. 'What about John? Is Rita back?'

'John's sleeping and Rita's happy, sitting with him.' Ben took her hand in his and turned them in the direction of the elevators. 'Let's go and find you some old art thing to take home for your apartment.'

'Old art thing? Very classy, Mr Wells.' But she had been intending to look at the antiques in the hope of finding a piece of porcelain to add to her growing collection.

'Absolutely, Tori.' His fingers squeezed hers gently.

At least he hadn't said Mrs Wells. She should pull away from his hand. Would do so in a minute. But not just yet. It had been too long since she'd had physical contact with Benji—she wouldn't count a kiss and a few other touches over the last few days—and she was learning how much she'd missed that. Not that she hadn't known, of course she had, but to touch him, have his hand in hers brought back memories of other intimacies. Intimacies she'd enjoyed. All this from a hand touch. Yes, Benji was getting to her—again.

His name is Ben. Ben, not Benji. Sure. Of course.

'I love that one.' Tori pointed to an urn tucked in the corner of a shop two hours later. 'I want to buy it.'

Ben stared at the nearly four-foot-tall urn and shook his head. 'Of course you do. Have you booked a spare seat on the plane?'

'Don't be difficult.' But it wouldn't be the easiest thing to get home. Not only big, but fragile to boot. 'I wonder if they package and deliver?'

'The extra seat might be cheaper,' Ben noted, even as he shifted a small chair to give her better access to her heart's desire.

'It's beautiful.' She sighed. Not the small piece of

porcelain she'd been thinking of finding. 'It's going to look perfect in the entranceway.' The multi shades of blue in the floral design would look stunning against the cream walls and the duck-egg-blue tiles of her foyer.

'You're serious, aren't you?' Ben was studying her urn. 'I only hope it survives the trip.' He headed to the man watching them from behind a wonderful carved wood counter and began trying to explain the situation.

Tori left him to it and sat on the chair to study the urn. Running her fingers lightly over the surface, she felt a thrill tingle up her spine. What an amazing souvenir to take home from France. If it was at all possible. Surely the shop owner would be used to sending his precious antiques all around the world? She'd be devastated if the urn arrived in pieces.

'Seems anything is possible,' Ben leaned down to tell her.

Turning her head, her eyes locked with his. 'Truly? That's wonderful.' She should be looking away, but for the life of her she couldn't drag her gaze from his twinkling caramel eyes. Eyes full of laughter and charm and— Love? For her? Couldn't be. 'Ben?'

He leaned closer, so that she could feel his breath on her cheek. Then his lips brushed her cheek, her mouth.

'*Madame*, you want this urn to go to New Zealand?'

Tori jerked back and stared around to find the shop owner watching her with amusement. 'Y-yes,' she stuttered. 'Is that possible?'

'It is. It will be very expensive for the freight,' the man told her.

'I expected that.'

'You haven't asked how much this will all cost,' Ben reminded her.

Too late. The man would have to be comatose not to

see that she'd pay just about anything to have it, and was probably upping the price right then. 'What's the price of the urn?' she asked anyway, because she did need to know sometime.

The man's English was clear and precise and they soon reached agreement on the price and then arranged freight and the insurance to cover any mishap on the way.

Back out on the street Ben said, 'I need a drink after that.' He took her hand again—she was getting used to this and liking it—and tugged her across the road into a wine bar.

After ordering sparkling water for her and beer for himself, Ben settled onto the chair opposite her. 'I thought you'd have moved out of that apartment once I'd gone.'

It's where my memories of you were freshest at the time. Memories I needed to get through long and lonely days, and to remind myself we had been in love once.

Memories that had helped her through the post-miscarriage blues a little, and at other times had dragged her down even deeper. 'It was in the perfect location and had everything I'd always wanted for my home so I had no reason to sell and move.'

The fact Ben had left her was more than enough reason, according to her friends, and they'd never understood why she'd hung on to the place. Sometimes when she'd been struggling to come to terms with his departure she'd questioned herself, had once gone as far as making an appointment with a real estate salesperson, which she'd cancelled at the last minute. She hadn't needed the added stress of selling, finding another home and moving.

'Have you redecorated, as you'd planned?'

As *they'd* planned. 'It's had a total refit, including a new state-of-the-art kitchen that I hardly get to use. Actually, I don't use the place much at all.'

'You spend all your time at work?' He sipped his beer.

Those lips that could do wild things to her skin fascinated her. Soft, firm, delicious, sensual. A shiver of pleasure tripped through her. Then the smile that had been hovering on her mouth slipped a little. He'd asked her something about work, hadn't he? 'Work? Time?' She shook her head. 'The clinic keeps me busy, plus I'm on the roster at the cardiac unit at Auckland Hospital.'

Ben sucked in a breath. 'Does working all the time make us a little crazy?'

She shrugged. 'I don't think about it.' Hadn't until today anyway. 'Though occasionally when I hear the staff talking about what they did over the weekend or the show they saw one night I wonder if I should try and get a life outside my career. But where to start? What to do? Seems too complicated.'

'What happened to Diane and Lynley?'

Her girlfriends from way back. 'They're both still in Auckland and about once a month they drag me out to a restaurant for a fabulous meal, or make me join them for a spa weekend.' *And nag at me for not dating and for working too hard and living a half life.* 'Tell me about living in London. That seems so exciting.' *And will divert you from asking about me.*

'Sometimes I've had to pinch myself to believe I actually live there amongst all the historical buildings and places I'd read about growing up. Then on other days when work's frantic and I hardly see more of my apartment than the bedroom and bathroom I think it's no different to living in Auckland or Sydney.' Ben turned his glass back and forth between his fingers. 'But I've learned to take regular breaks away. That's when I go explore different parts of Britain.'

Regular breaks. 'We were working hideous hours.' Longer even than what she did nowadays.

'I can't blame that for what happened, Tori. I stuffed up in that operation and a woman died because I thought I knew better than anyone else how to do that procedure. There is no other way of looking at it.' He was watching her intently. Looking for what?

Surprised that he was even talking about that day, she didn't look away, instead watched him back. 'Operations go wrong. It's a fact of life and why patients sign a declaration before surgery.'

'That doesn't let me off the hook.' Ben didn't sound bitter at all. More like resigned.

'Have you forgiven yourself?'

'No.' He gulped at his beer. 'But I have accepted that I made that error through my own ego. I wanted the kudos that would've gone with success.'

He'd have wanted his father's praise more than anything.

'I don't have much contact with my father any more.'

Had he read her mind? Tori reached across and took his free hand in both hers, her thumbs rubbing softly back and forth across his warm skin. 'That's sad.'

'Yes and no. It was like a huge weight coming off my shoulders when I realised how often I'd done things to make him proud, only to be given an offhand nod and told to do better with the next project. I should've wised up and done something about that a long time before. Pathetic to be in my thirties and still trying to please my parents.'

'If only I'd known what had really happened right from the outset.' He hadn't told her, had refused point-blank whenever she'd asked, so that eventually they'd stopped talking completely, drawing apart increment by increment, so that their marriage had felt empty. 'Why didn't you tell me the whole story?'

Ben drained his glass, set it down with a bang. 'I was too ashamed.'

Her heart rolled. Hurt glittered out at her. Ben ashamed? 'Enough not to talk to me? When the whole hospital was talking, making up unknown facts?'

'I thought you'd despise me. We were both so good at what we did, I didn't want you to look down on me.' He looked away, swallowed hard. Looked back. 'Can you understand that?'

'Not really, because I never would've felt like that.' Was this why their marriage had failed? Because he'd believed she'd despise him for making a mistake? A terrible error, granted, but the point being it had been a mistake. 'Not when I think of how our lives unravelled afterwards.' Though their marriage had already been faltering before that.

He pulled his hand away. 'I should've talked to you, explained everything that happened that day. But every time I tried to the words failed me. You were my other half, my rock, my love, and I'd screwed up big time. I couldn't bear to think you'd be disgusted with me for a mistake that you'd never make.'

'Hell, Ben, I'd never have thought that.' It wouldn't have occurred to her. He hadn't known her as well as she'd thought if he believed that. 'You know, I heard so much gossip that the plain truth from you would've been a hundred times better than what I was being slammed with every day.'

'I know.' He looked around for the waitress, then indicated another round.

She hadn't drunk half her water yet, but chose not to point that out. It had taken a long time to have this conversation and now she didn't know what to make of it. 'You didn't trust my love.'

His hands slapped the tabletop. 'I was protecting myself, my heart. Not a good reason to stop talking to you, I know, but that's how it was.'

'Ben…' Ben, what? She reached for her glass, drank deeply of the refreshing liquid. If only he'd talked to her, they could've faced this together, come up with a solution for their futures together. But he hadn't, and there was no going back and rewriting their history. Marriage was about love, yes, but equally about sharing, and being up-front and talking.

Yeah, and you're saying you didn't give up trying to communicate with Ben? You drank to drown out your problems, instead of facing them together. And what about the important news you didn't tell him? You were no better at communication.

'What a mess we made of things.' She drained her glass and reached for the new one.

'Thanks for saying "we", but—'

'But nothing,' she interrupted. 'Maybe we weren't ready to be married, weren't as committed as we believed. If we had been we'd have got through those awful months. All couples face difficulties, have to deal with ghastly things, and most get through it—together. We didn't. We screwed up, to use your phrase.' Shoving the glass aside, Tori stood up. 'I'm sorry but I've had enough.'

She headed for the street and walked along blindly, tears tracking down her face. Not once did she glance backwards to see if Ben had followed her. He was probably still sitting in the café, nursing his beer.

Tori turned corners willy-nilly until she was completely lost. Who cared? Not her. Even when her feet
began to ache she continued trudging up and down the
streets. The tears dried up, the ache in her throat less-
ened, but her heart remained as heavy as a bucket of
concrete.

*Damn you, Benji. I loved you. But we didn't have what
it takes to make a good, strong marriage. Which means
we still don't, so get out of my head, my heart, and let
me get on with my life. Let me drop this silly notion that
we might have a chance at getting back together.*

But it was getting harder by the minute to keep
Benji at arm's length. Because she did want that second
chance.

Ben watched Tori slow down and finally stop her crazy
racing around the streets. She sat down at an outdoor
table at a café she'd stumbled across. He knew she was
lost. The woman had never had any sense of direction,
which was why he'd followed her when she'd stormed
off. Sure, a taxi would get her back to the hotel, no
trouble, but she'd been upset and he'd wanted to keep
an eye on her.

He approached the waiter hovering in the café entrance and ordered two coffees before crossing to join
Tori. 'You done yet?' he asked.

Her head jerked upwards. 'What are you doing here?'

Her eyes were red and her face swollen from crying.
What had brought those tears on? They'd been talking about the sensitive stuff, sure, but he wouldn't have
thought any of it warranted a crying spell.

'Making sure you were okay.' When she didn't send
him away he pulled out a chair and dropped onto it. 'But
you're not, are you?'

She looked away. Her finger began picking at a spot on the table. 'I'm good.'

'Tori, this is me you're trying to convince. Try again.'

It seemed an age before she sighed and lifted her gaze to his. Guilt glittered out at him. 'I'm so sorry, Ben.'

Apprehension had him sitting up a little straighter. What could Tori have done to produce that guilt?

Her eyes darkened and she looked away again. 'That night you came back to pack up the last of your things?' She came back to watching him.

He gave a sharp nod. 'Go on.'

Silence stretched out between them. Tori's hands were still, too still. Her teeth were biting her bottom lip so hard it was white. Then people at a nearby table started talking loudly and Tori said in a rush, 'I was in hospital. I had a miscarriage.'

'What?' he roared. A miscarriage? Tori? He hadn't known she was pregnant. That they were having a baby. She hadn't told him. Anger began tightening his belly, hot and hard. This was the woman he'd put on a pedestal, had believed too honest for her own good sometimes. 'You didn't tell me.'

'I wanted to.'

'Your phone wasn't working?'

She flinched. 'I deserve that.'

He'd spent years regretting the fact he hadn't told her exactly what had happened that day in Theatre, had felt guilty for keeping his shame under wraps. And all along Tori had been keeping quiet about something equally important. 'If you hadn't miscarried, would you have told me you were pregnant?'

'Of course.' She looked aghast.

'There's no "of course" about it. You didn't tell me about the miscarriage or that you were pregnant.'

'I didn't know until I started bleeding and had stomach cramps the likes of which I'd never had before.' The guilt in her eyes had been replaced with sorrow.

He had to steel his heart against reaching for her and soothing away her sadness. Despite the anger boiling in his gut, despite the sense of having been let down big time, he wanted to soothe her? Hell, man, what was his problem?

Their coffees arrived. Neither of them touched the steaming mugs.

Tori continued in that muted tone he hated. 'My periods were always erratic, and at the time, with so much going on, I hadn't noticed I hadn't had one for months.'

'Just how far along were you when you miscarried?'

'About nine weeks, or so the doctors said.'

'Were we having a boy or a girl?' Why ask? It didn't change a thing, only added to the hurt by making it more real.

'Too soon to tell.' Again her teeth bit down hard on her lip. It must've been hurting but she didn't stop. Her eyelids were opening and shutting rapidly. Fighting tears? Fair enough. Tori would still grieve for her baby. She hadn't changed that much.

Ben fought the urge to get up and run. Run hard and fast to pound away this feeling of hanging over a canyon. That Tori had been hiding something so important from him was unfathomable. His gut clenched tighter, sweat ran down his back. 'Why didn't you tell me?'

'You'd left me and I was reeling with the shock... No. Sorry. That's an excuse. I didn't want you coming back just because you felt like you had to help me through the aftermath of the miscarriage.'

She had a point. He would've insisted on staying with

her until she was back on her feet. But, 'I was entitled to be there for you. That was *our* baby, not just yours.'

The face she turned to him was grief-stricken. 'You think I don't realise that? That I don't feel guilty about losing our baby? I was so ashamed I couldn't bring myself to tell you.'

She held out her wrist, showing him the gold bracelet that she never took off. Her voice shook as she choked out, 'I had this bracelet made in memory of our baby. Don't think for a second that I haven't thought about our baby every single day since it happened.'

'I don't know what to think any more. I'm still getting to grips with the fact you kept this secret in the first place.' He had to get away, couldn't sit here like a civilised man, trying to absorb what had gone down. His chair crashed over as he leapt to his feet. 'Did I ever really know you, Tori?'

She gasped. Then reached for her coffee, slopped it everywhere before banging the cup back down. 'I am so sorry, Ben. More than you can ever know.'

He was gone. Charging down the pavement heading for who knew where. Anywhere as long as it was away from Tori. He couldn't bear to face her, to see her guilt and apology in those eyes that had always sucked him in. Because he did know about being sorry. Did know about not talking about the important things between them. He'd been carrying the same guilt for just as long.

To think he'd wanted to try again with her. Like that was going to happen now when neither of them could trust the other to be completely honest.

Toot, toot. Screech.

Hell. He'd stepped off the footpath onto the road, directly in front of a car. 'Sorry, mate,' he called at the cursing driver. 'My fault entirely.' Like the guy could understand him.

On the opposite side of the road was a bar. Ben changed direction slightly, aiming for the door and his first French hangover.

CHAPTER EIGHT

BEN'S HAND WAS on Tori's elbow as he led the way through the jostling crowd and out of the Paris railway station to the taxi rank. She knew he'd feel her trembling. As long as he recognised that as excitement over being in this amazing city and not the desperation and guilt she hadn't been able to overcome since her big revelation to him yesterday.

He'd surprised her by touching her. He hadn't spoken more than was absolutely necessary on the long trip up from Nice, and had spent most of the day staring out the window or reading something on his tablet. It had been as though she'd been like all the other passengers—a stranger he'd had no interest in whatsoever.

Fair enough. She'd had it coming. But why Ben had insisted on joining her on the train and not flying to Paris, as he'd originally planned, was beyond her. Did it mean he might be thawing towards her? Or was she overreacting because the excitement of being in Paris was getting to her?

'Paris.' Tori breathed deep. Parisian air. She would not be daunted by Ben's attitude, either way. 'I want to squeal and dance up and down on the spot.'

He shook his head at her. 'I bet you do.'

You're a grown-up and grown-ups don't do that.

Tori jumped up and down on the spot, squealing loudly, 'I'm in Paris. Whoopee.' Around her some people laughed and cheered, others pretended there wasn't a mad woman let loose at Gare du Nord.

Ben watched her, his eyes hooded, his mouth flat.

She poked him. 'No matter what I've done in the past I am not going to spend my time in Paris scowling.' *Like you.*

His mouth twitched.

'Go on. You can do it, and it won't hurt, promise,' she teased.

A smile slowly spread over his face, lifting his lips, lightening those eyes that had been dark and distressed all day. He shook his head at her. 'This is only the railway station, one of many railway stations.'

'It's a Paris railway station. We don't have those at home.'

His eyebrows rose as he nodded briefly. 'I can't argue with your logic.'

'I've dreamed of coming here since I was knee-high to a grasshopper. Nothing can dampen the most amazing moment of my life.' His smile slipped and she hastened to add, 'Make that one of the most amazing moments.' Even now, despite everything, her wedding day took the top award for that.

'Let's go and get checked in at the hotel so we can see more of your dream city.' His fingers were back on her elbow as he turned her in the direction of an available taxi.

'Bring it on.' *I'm in Paris with Ben.* Definitely Ben today, not Benji. But she could pretend he was Benji and that they were a couple. Setting herself up for a fall?

The hotel had been arranged for them by Luc. One of the best, they'd been assured. Not that she usually went for top-notch hotels but, hey, this was Paris, and she was with Ben. Hopefully they'd get past their difficulties enough to enjoy the time they spent here together.

Sitting in the taxi, her head turned left, right, then to the front. She was afraid she'd miss something. 'There's so much to take in. Oh, my gosh, there's the top of the Eiffel Tower.' She could barely see it above a line of trees. Pinching herself, she gaped at the sight until it disappeared behind the beautiful old buildings lining the street they'd turned into.

Ben's smile had disappeared but he did seem more relaxed than he had been. 'You sure five days are going to be enough to see everything you want?'

'Five weeks wouldn't be enough. Look at you. You're supposed to checking out the passing sights, not staring at me.' It was as though he got more fun out of her reactions to the city than to the city itself. But, then, he'd been here before.

Pulling up outside the grandest hotel she'd been to, her sense of excitement only increased. The hotel was very close to the Seine and many of the attractions she planned on visiting. Strolling inside with Ben, Tori realised she hadn't felt this happy for a long time, and knew it wasn't all to do with being in this city.

At the reception desk her happiness evaporated instantly. 'But there's been some mistake,' she gulped, staring at the swipe key for the same suite as Ben was using. She would not share with him. She might've agreed to spend time with him but she wasn't ready to be twenty-four seven in his company. Though a part of her wanted to. To test the waters, so to speak.

'You are Monsieur and Madame Wells? We were told to book you into one of our best suites. It has two bedrooms, two bathrooms, views out across the city. What more can you want?' The receptionist looked perplexed.

Tori asked, 'Is there another room available?'

'Yes, we have a single room on the third floor.'

'That will do nicely.'

Ben shook his head. 'Tori, the apartment has two bedrooms so it's not as though we'll be sharing *everything*.'

She shook her head. She'd feel his presence even with her bedroom door shut, would be straining to hear him moving about, and wanting to talk to him. Wondering how he felt about her now that he knew about the baby that they'd lost.

'Okay, I'll take the third-floor room.' Ben shrugged. 'The one with the view of the back of a building.' He actually smiled of his own free will. 'While you have the views of Paris with the iconic sights.'

'Dirty tactics,' she replied, trying to bite down on the smile that was threatening to break out. Hard to be down in this city.

'Of course.' He seemed to be waiting for her to make up her mind.

She'd love those views. How could she banish Ben to the basement, so to speak? It wasn't as though he'd made the booking for them. No, Monsieur Leclare had undertaken to find them a very good hotel with very good rooms. What the heck? She'd give the suite a go and if the situation became too difficult or tense she'd find another room or hotel. Who knew? Now that there were no secrets between them, it might be the catalyst needed to get them back together. If that was at all possible. There were times when she thought it was, then yesterday and today she'd known it wasn't. 'Come on. Let's go upstairs to our suite and dump our bags. Paris is waiting.'

The city of love. Tori hummed the words over and over as she wandered along the bank of the Seine. More than once she caught herself reaching for Ben's hand, wanting to entwine her fingers between his, pulling back just before her fingers touched him. Unsurprisingly, his mood hadn't thawed that much.

'Let's go down one of those narrow streets and find a café where we can enjoy a drink on the sidewalk while people-watching.' Ben was already heading for the other side of the street.

'Good idea,' she muttered at his back.

Within moments they'd found a line of cafés and Tori happily sank onto a chair at a minuscule table out in the sun. 'This is what I always dreamt Paris would be like.'

Ben bought sparkling water and beer with cheese sticks before joining her. 'I've been in Paris twice but never done this.'

'You're joking.' How could anyone not do this?

'It wouldn't have been half the fun on my own.' There was no hidden meaning in his voice, though maybe a hint of sadness.

'I don't know. There'd be so much going on you'd have to be enthralled.' Listening in on a French couple's conversation at the next table, she sighed with content- ment and leaned close to Ben. 'He's told her the car needs a new battery.' She grinned. 'How's that? I un- derstood him.'

Ben shook his head at her. 'You've come all this way to eavesdrop on some poor, unsuspecting guy's talk with his wife?'

'Absolutely.' Sipping her water, she continued lis- tening in.

'When did you give up drinking alcohol?'

She spluttered water down her front. 'After the miscarriage.' She lifted imploring eyes to him. *Can we leave it at that?* But deep down she knew it was something they needed to talk about, in order to move forwards.

'You're not blaming your drinking for the miscarriage?' Shock resonated between them.

Splutter. At this rate she'd spray most of her water over the pavement and get little down her throat. 'Yes. Of course I am.'

'You can't say categorically the alcohol was the cause. It could've been nature, or the immense strain you were under, no thanks to me.' Ben wasn't holding back. Had the atmosphere of the city of love touched him, loosened his tongue? Or had learning of their baby make him think he was free to talk about anything and everything?

'I realised that I'd been drinking to numb myself, instead of talking to you about how I was feeling.' The glass shook in her hand as she tried to gulp some water. 'If I'd even suspected I was pregnant I'd never have touched a drop.'

'It must have been awful, Tori. I'm sorry that I wasn't there for you. I suspected you were drinking too much, but I turned a blind eye, because I knew I was the cause of you being so unhappy.' She could only stare at him and shake her head at the fact that it had taken Ben a while to truly understand that hurt.

'Tori? Have I gone too far?'

'Yes.' This was making her sad, which was the last thing she wanted. 'Look, Ben, how about we leave the past alone and make the most of being here? Nothing contentious to be discussed.' She was afraid they'd have another meltdown and she didn't want that happening here. Or anywhere, if she thought about it.

'Deal.'

* * *

Ben stretched his legs out under the table, sipped his beer, fully aware of the hangover only just fading away, and aimed for relaxed. It wasn't easy. He wanted to be with Tori, but he still hadn't been able to get the baby out of his head, and, worse, Tori's deception still rankled. He knew he had to get past that. One day at a time had just become his new motto. He was more than happy to comply with Tori's edict. The past could stay there— for now. Digging into that brought up live bombs he had no idea how to defuse without carnage. So the next few days were about moving forward and finally letting Tori go. It didn't seem so impossible now, as any idea of trying to make a go of their relationship had gone out the window yesterday.

Thank goodness they both had their own agendas to get back to. This was only an interlude. Tori had too much at stake with so many children relying on her. He'd focus on working towards that partnership he desperately needed to prove to himself he was better than that cocky surgeon he'd been, stuffing up so badly in Auckland. Nothing short of a partnership in the clinic at Harley Street would make him happy. It was there, dangling in front of him so he could almost taste it. He just had to be patient.

'Where have you gone?' Tori peered at him through her sunshades.

'Taking a break from thinking,' he fibbed.

'What shall we do tonight?'

'Wait and see.' He'd booked them a table for dinner on a river boat so they could see the city at night. A relaxed way to finish their day. 'Dress in your evening finery, that's all I'm saying.'

Her eyes lit up with fun. 'When did you plan whatever we're doing?'

'Before we checked out of the hotel this morning.' Even when he'd still been angry with her he'd still wanted to make her time in Paris special. Had he gone soft in the head? Probably.

'Thank you.' Her hand was warm on his.

The river cruise turned out to be fun and beautiful and romantic. Ben hadn't factored in dancing on the deck to a five-piece orchestra. With Tori in his arms he could've stayed there all night. He hadn't allowed for her looking stunning in a cream, fitted dress that stopped short of her knees, highlighting her slim legs and all those gorgeous curves. He hadn't considered how he might have to control his runaway hormones and the deep, almost crippling need to make love to her.

'I can't believe I'm here,' Tori whispered, as he led her around a couple who'd stopped to kiss. 'With you,' she added.

This was so not how he'd planned on winding up their relationship for good. 'It is magic,' he agreed, because it would be rude not to. And he couldn't think of anything else to say without spoiling her mood.

Warmth brushed his neck. Tori had kissed him—on that exact spot just under his chin that always turned him on fast. Deliberately? Had she remembered? Why would she? Why wouldn't she?

The boat nudged against the wharf. With a dry mouth and thudding heart he put her away from him. It was midnight. 'Come on, Cinderella, time we were back at the hotel.' The hotel where they shared a suite of opulent rooms and the same air. Not that Tori would ever turn into anything remotely resembling a pumpkin but he had all his fingers crossed he didn't turn into an idiot with a pole in the front of his trousers hindering his walking back to the hotel.

As they stepped onto land Tori slid her hand into his and cuddled closer. *Damn woman, how can I remain impervious to you? You are such a turn-on.*

'What time are we expected at the medical school tomorrow?' he asked in a pathetic attempt to quieten his racing heart.

Her head twisted against his arm as she glanced up at him. 'Nine o'clock.' Her smile zoomed straight to his toes, scorching every inch of his body on the way past, and did nothing to help his situation. 'I know you haven't forgotten. You forget nothing.'

'I forgot your birthday once.' Would that cool the air?

'No, you didn't want to wake me up when you got home late at night because I'd just finished a sixteen-hour shift.' Her smile widened, and then she tripped because she wasn't looking where she was going, and he was catching her and holding her close.

'You were exhausted.' Her length pressed against him. Now he'd definitely be in trouble. There was no denying his need for her pushing into her belly.

Tori stretched up on tiptoe and placed that beautiful mouth against his. Her tongue slipped inside to taste him and all his good intentions dissolved in a flash of heat and desire and longing so deep it hurt.

'Tori,' he groaned against her lips. 'I've missed you something terrible.' What had happened to moving on?

Her kiss deepened. Her arms wrapped around him, her hands joined at the back of his neck, pulling him closer—if that was possible. Those sweet breasts he remembered so well flattened against his chest. Under his hands her buttocks were soft globes of heat. If his heart didn't explode out of his chest it would beat itself to death against his ribs.

'Ben,' she whispered, and then returned to kissing him.

He stopped thinking and focused entirely on Tori and deepening that kiss. Until he ran out of oxygen. Pulling back, he dragged in a load of air and returned to her mouth.

The street sweepers would probably have found them still kissing in the early morning if a group from the cruise hadn't walked past, making loud, lurid comments at their expense.

Tori tensed, then turned in his arms to glare after them. 'Sad puppies.' She leaned back and folded her arms across her waist. Tried to keep air between her butt and his very obvious need.

Ben laid his chin on the top of her head and breathed in the combined scent of Tori and the city. Paradise. That's where he was right now. Torturous paradise. Would this…? *Stop overthinking everything. Stop thinking at all.*

Tori broke away and asked, 'Do you mind if we walk a while? I'm not ready for sleep.'

Disappointment surged even though he knew she had done the right thing. He wanted her, suspected she felt the same, but falling into bed together wasn't going bring him closure. Or would it? Who was he kidding? But Tori had to be willing. That kiss suggested she might be but he wouldn't push the advantage. One step at a time. And not making love to Tori might save his heart. But going ahead might help him to stop wondering what it would be like to make love to her once more.

Tori dropped her arms to her sides and stepped out along the pavement. 'You'll have to keep track of where we are. I don't relish getting lost.'

They walked in silence for a while. The night was warm and the streets busy despite the late hour.

Then Tori said, 'Ben, about that kiss, I shouldn't have. But I couldn't help myself. You were there, warm and distracting, being Benji.'

If he'd thought he was handling this situation with aplomb, he needed to think again. Now he felt gutted. And hurt. 'I'm not going to drag you into my bed when we get back to our suite, if that's what's worrying you.'

'I'm not worried about a thing, Ben. I'm apologising for not showing any restraint.' Her chin tilted upwards and her eyes held his. 'For not following up on your re-action to me.'

A direct hit. 'I'm a red-blooded man. You're a beau-tiful, sexy woman. It would've been rude of me not to react.'

She smiled.

If only there was more light for him to read her clearly. He thought he saw longing reflected in her gaze, but that could've been wishful thinking on his part. 'We agreed to enjoy our time here, and it's not always going to be easy for us. In more ways than one.' He jammed his hands deep in his pockets and began walking again, moving more quickly than before. He needed to get to the hotel and his room so he could put some space be-tween them. Not that it would be easy, knowing she was only through the door. He liked it that she hadn't been totally in control. It was also best that she'd found some before they did go too far.

'Want to walk all night?' There was no way he'd be falling asleep tonight.

'That's a no from me.' Her laugh warmed him all the way to his toes and did nothing to relieve the ten-sion inside him.

CHAPTER NINE

TORI CLOSED HER emails, worry gnawing at her. Dean was not responding to the antibiotics he'd been given for his strep throat. His third strep throat in weeks.

'What's up?' Ben strolled through from his room, looking good enough to eat with his shirt open, exposing his sculpted chest.

Do your buttons up. Now. Before I make an idiot of myself again. Bare chests and remaining impervious don't go together, and it would be best for both of us if I remain aloof from you and your sexy body. Except... If we are finally being honest and open with each other, does it mean there is hope for us? As a couple again?

Her heart hammered in her chest. That would come with a load of logistical problems, but if they wanted it badly enough they could sort those.

Ben was looking at her strangely. What had she been talking about? A glance at her phone and she was back on track. 'I'm worried about Dean. I put an assist device into his left ventricle before I came away.' She clicked back into her mail and found the photo Dean had sent her days ago. 'Look at him. The picture of health.'

'So where's the problem?' Two steps closer to her and Ben's aftershave was taunting her.

'The other day I had him recalled after learning that

he's not sleeping. He's got another strep throat. Not uncommon for Dean.'

'Do you think he has another underlying problem?' Ben asked.

'It's possible. Or the procedure hasn't worked properly and we have to repeat it.' She moved across the room to put space between them. That masculine scent followed her. Her body ached from lack of sleep. Or was it the tossing and turning she'd done while fighting the urge to visit Ben in his bed? Only the sensible part of her brain had kept her in her own bed. 'Maybe I should go home early.'

Ben crossed to stand directly in front of her, his very presence forcing her to look up. Those eyes that had drilled her brain all night were filled with concern. For her? 'Is that really what you want to do? You don't trust your staff to get this right?'

Her spine stiffened. 'Of course I know the others can handle it, but I feel responsible. Dean's parents moved their family from Dunedin to Auckland so I could treat their son. I should be there for them.'

'Tori, you don't have to take on guilt for a decision they made. That will only wear you down.'

'You might be right but that doesn't make it any easier.' The time and effort she put into her patients did take its toll. This was the first real break she'd had since opening the clinic.

'Why don't you arrange for the parents to come online to talk to you while the other doctors are with them?'

'Good idea.' She was all out of those at the moment. Tiredness and the mammoth distraction Ben was to her equilibrium had knocked her for six. And she still wanted to kiss him again.

'I could listen in, if that's a help.'

'Would you? I'd like that.' Togetherness.

'Set up a time now.' He glanced at his watch. 'If the parents are there we've still got an hour before we have to leave for the hospital.'

'That might be rushing things. Dean's parents live on the North Shore. But we could talk to Conrad now anyway.' She stepped around him, maintaining that distance she needed between them, and quickly sent an email to Conrad. Only minutes passed before Conrad's face was filling her screen.

Tori introduced the men. 'Conrad, Ben Wells is a cardiac surgeon in London.' She saw the man blink when she gave Ben's surname. He'd be able to put two and two together and come up with some answer close to the truth. 'Ben's done lots of these procedures.'

Ben leaned forward. 'Hello, Conrad. Do you mind if I ask a few questions about Dean's health? Tori has filled me in on the procedure and it sounds as though it was straightforward with no complications.'

'Go ahead. I should tell you Dean is showing similar symptoms to those he presented before we operated.'

Tori tried to lean sideways, away from Ben, but it didn't work. Too far from Ben meant too far from the screen. 'It's not post-op exhaustion, is it?'

'Is the wound completely healed?' Ben asked.

'There's no inflammation. Dean says the pain's gone. But he's wide-awake and totally exhausted at the same time. His mum is beside herself with worry.' Conrad looked equally worried. 'I've requested bloods and microbiology to see if he's got an infection at the operation site.'

'Ben wondered if Dean has something else going on that would make him unwell. What do you think?' Tori asked.

'Everything points to how he was before surgery but I'll add some more tests to be done at the lab. Can't be too careful.'

Tori knew Conrad could do this, would know what had to be done, and had others to call on. But she found it hard not being there, even when knowing she was entitled to time off and that she'd left everything in good hands. There were other specialists from a major private practice using the same private hospital facilities she used who were there for Conrad and the other staff.

Stifling her anxiety, she said to him, 'Let me know those results when you get them and keep me up-to-date on any changes in Dean's condition. You might be looking at having to repeat the procedure. If Dean's parents have any issues, set them up to talk to me tonight.'

'Will do.'

The screen went blank.

'Your young man might be in for a heart transplant if the procedure is working properly,' Ben warned her.

She shuddered. 'I hate the thought. But the alternative is worse.' Heart transplants were one of medicine's miracles, but she still had a hard time removing a badly diseased, barely functioning one to replace it with a healthy donated one. It was that time lapse between the patient not having his or her own heart and relying on a machine to stay alive until the replacement one was beating that twisted her stomach into more knots than found on a macramé rug. Once the new heart was working correctly and the patient was coming round, she always finally relaxed enough to breathe properly and let the tension out of her muscles. Her body paid for the strain for days afterwards. And she was only the doctor. It was so much worse for the recipient and the families.

'Let's not think too long on that path and focus on

easier alternatives until you know differently.' Ben folded his arms across his chest. Thank goodness the buttons were done up now. 'No looking too far ahead, remember?'

Was he talking about Dean or them? As far as their relationship went, she couldn't stop wondering if they could make it work second time round. Her hormones were behaving erratically, reminding her all the time how they'd like nothing more than to play with Ben's. See? She missed his body the moment he'd stepped away. It would be so easy to lean in against that hard, muscular physique and let him brush aside her worries. Like he used to. Not going to happen. But she'd come very close to slipping into his room and curling up against, and around, him during the night.

What would he think if he knew? He'd returned her kiss ardently last night, and had seemed to regret it when they'd stopped. Regret it? Come on, the guy had had an erection that had been impossible to miss.

Snatching up her handbag, she dug deep amongst the clutter for a lipstick. She'd put that on and then get out of here. Ben would still be with her but they'd be amongst other doctors and the conversation would be generic. Not laced with longing and double entendres.

They were sitting in a taxi, bound for the teaching wing of one of the city's major hospitals, when Ben tipped her world sideways. Again. 'Would you ever consider leaving the clinic and coming over this way to live?'

It took minutes before she could breathe evenly and find some words for him. Even then they were hardly startling. 'No. Why?'

'Just reminding myself of the impossibility of our situation.'

'Are you playing games with me?' she snapped. Guess she knew where she stood, then.

'Not intentionally.' Ben leaned back into the corner and stared out the window. 'I'm not going to lie, Tori. I was angry when you told me about the baby. You, the most forthright woman I know, hadn't bothered to tell me at the time.'

Her hands gripped the handle of her bag like a lifeline as she fought to remain calm and reasoned in her reply—if she could get one out around her dry tongue stuck in her dry mouth. 'Your point being?' she eventually managed.

He continued. 'It's ironic, really. If I hadn't felt so bad for hiding the truth from you I might not have left and we might still be married.' Ben was still staring beyond the taxi.

She found her voice. 'Then I'd have told you I was pregnant the moment I found out—which was the night I lost her.' Tori dug deep for calm, swallowing the guilt his comments had raised. Guess that would take a long time to go away completely. 'What happened to living these days in Paris in the here and now?'

'I never was good at sticking to the rules.' He didn't even smile, let alone look at her.

A memory sprang into her mind. *Staff are not to use storerooms for anything other than storage.* Finding a nurse or doctor who hadn't had a liaison in a storeroom at some time would be as easy as finding a five-legged cat. She and Ben had liked the linen room behind the cardiology ward sluice room. The chances of being interrupted had been small and no one could approach without being heard on the floor kept particularly clean and squeaky for that reason. 'Some rules are a waste of time even putting out there.'

'But not this one. I get it.' Odd that he gave her a smile then, giving her the sense that he was embarking on some adventure and she was the focus of all his intentions. Or had she got that wrong? Fingers crossed.

Time to put a stop to this and get the day at the university going. 'I want to make the most of my days here and not have to think all the time about what's going on with you and me.' If he believed that he didn't have a clue to the state of her mind, and Ben was no slug. He'd know all right. 'If that means avoiding each other, then that's what we'll do.'

His finger touched the back of her hand on the seat between them. 'We'll stick to the plan.'

Tori smiled softly. 'The plan. Sounds a bit serious, doesn't it?' It was serious. As was the disappointment over Ben readily agreeing to it, even when that's exactly what she needed. Talk about taking a ride in a spin-dryer. Round and round, up and down. Her emotions were all over the show. Talking of shows... 'What time does the show at the Moulin Rouge start?'

'Eleven. It's the late show so I thought we could have dinner somewhere special first.' His finger had gone, leaving a warm spot on her hand.

'I am really looking forward to the evening. Monsieur Leclare is wonderful, getting us seats at such short notice.'

'I understand he has someone on the inside who often helps him out.' Ben glanced out the window. 'Here we are. This should prove to be an interesting morning. If French medical students are as exhausted and overworked as the ones in New Zealand, we'll have to be really interesting or they'll all fall asleep during our talks.'

Tori laughed and told him, 'We could make up some ridiculous procedure to keep them interested.'

'Like, this man needs a heart transplant, Doctor? Then you're in luck. I know where there are some stray pigs.'

See? They were in sync, some of the time anyway.

Ben climbed out of the taxi and held his hand out to her. 'Think you can direct us to the director's office with your knowledge of French?'

She ignored his hand. Childish, maybe, but safer. Inside the main doors she read the board giving the locations for all the departments. 'We head left.'

And then left, right, along, left, left and right.

'I knew that board was written in Chinese,' Ben grumped as they turned yet another corner.

'Then I'm very proficient in that language because there's the office we want.' Reading the signs had been slightly easier than asking directions and having to listen to rapid-fire answers in French. But only slightly.

'That's my woman. Clever clogs.'

My woman? He'd had a slip of concentration to be saying that. But Tori had that irrational urge to leap up and down on the spot again. This time she managed to restrain herself, which was just as well because explaining her childlike antics to Luc, who was emerging from the office they were destined for, would have been more than embarrassing.

But, honestly, her emotions were seesawing. She wanted to remain impervious to Ben, but loved it that he made her feel so warm and fuzzy and good.

I'm falling in love with him all over again. She gasped. When Ben turned to stare at her she shook her head to rid it of that thought just in case his mind-reading skills were on full alert. *How can I fall in love with him when I never really fell out of love with him?*

Not that it was going to get her anywhere. Ben had

been at pains to prove he wasn't interested. So why return her kiss? Why the reaction to it?

'*Bonjour*, Heart Lady and Ben. Welcome to our teaching hospital.' Luc air-kissed her cheeks, then turned to Ben, his hand out in welcome. 'How's your friend John?'

'He was very talkative when I called him this morning. A good sign. His doctors are suggesting he can move to London in a day or two.' They were being overly cautious, probably because he was one of them. Thankfully John hadn't put up any argument and seemed happy to go along with whatever he was told to do. 'He's had a big shock, and I think he's still working his way around how lucky he is.'

Luc nodded. 'It takes time. Then he'll be wanting to rush around doing so much in case he has another attack and misses out on life.' Indicating they should follow him, he continued, 'We'll go across to the lecture hall where the students are awaiting your arrival.'

He led them back to where they'd come from, taking a much shorter route.

'Definitely Chinese,' Ben muttered to Tori. 'This guy's got it sussed.'

Her quick, controlled smile told him she'd got herself together again. What had caused that stunned-mullet look on her face minutes ago? Talk about a mixed page, impossible to read with any accuracy. Now, *there* was something different. He'd always known what Tori had been thinking, almost before she'd thought it, but, then, she hadn't wanted to hide anything from him back then.

They stepped out into the sunshine briefly before finding themselves in another massive building and being led into an amphitheatre full of people. The noise level was deafening and completely unintelligible to him.

Ben felt Tori hesitate, saw her shoulders tighten and then she stepped into the fray.

Luc introduced them to their interpreter. 'These students are so excited about you coming to talk to them. You won't hear a whisper once you start speaking.'

Ben felt uncomfortable at the accolades Luc laid on about him. Yes, Tori was awesome and deserved every word, but not him. He'd never be entitled to such praise, not when a family still grieved for their mother, wife and sister because of his error. He thought of that woman a lot, but more so since he'd caught up with Tori again. No doubt because the woman had been part of what had been the final straw in their disintegrating marriage.

'Students, put your hands together for Mr Ben Wells from London, and before that New Zealand. Which for some of you I need to explain is a very small country at the bottom of the globe.' Luc waited for the clapping to stop, then added, 'Unfortunately they're very good at rugby.'

The room erupted into good-natured laughter and, standing at the lectern, Ben joined in. When he could be heard he said, 'Wait until you hear Madame Tori Wells talk, then you'll really understand how fanatic we Kiwis are about the game.'

'I think we already know,' Luc muttered close to the microphone, and got another laugh from his students. This was a more relaxed director than the man who'd been overseeing the conference. Here he was not only in charge but had the knowledge and experience this roomful of people hoped to gain. This was his patch.

Ben cleared his throat and began. 'I'm going to digress from the original talk for a moment. In London we are just starting to use hearts that haven't been kept pumping in brain-dead donors for transplant operations.

This is a very new and innovative procedure with so much potential for saving lives it's mind-blowing.

'These hearts are retrieved from post-mortem patients and are reactivated in what is called the heart-in-a-box machine. The heart is kept warm, the heartbeat is restored and then a fluid is used to reduce damage to the muscle.' He had the students entranced right from the get-go. No surprise there. It was exciting medicine. 'Hearts that have stopped beating for up to twenty minutes have been used in this technique.'

Winding up, Ben told his audience, 'This is edge-of-the-seat medicine, exciting and glamorous—if it goes well. It is also not for the faint-hearted. The potential for things to go wrong is huge and terrifying, not only for the patient but for the surgeons. Once the operation is started there is no going back.' One thing to come out of his error in Auckland was that he laboured the point with anyone who'd listen about keeping a clear head and the facts straight and constantly up-to-date. 'This kind of surgery is very intense, as is all surgery. The rewards are beyond explanation, and are why I do what I do.'

There. He'd laid his heart on the line in front hundreds of eager young people. But it was Tori he turned to. There were tears in the eyes she raised to his. Her smile was quivery and arrowed straight to his heart. She was clapping as hard as anyone in the room, and was the only applause he wanted.

Luc was on his feet. 'Thank you, Mr Wells. I know everyone here was as enthralled as I was to hear what's happening in your field.'

Ben acknowledged the audience with a wave before sitting down beside Tori. 'Now for the star of the show,' he said softly just beside her cute little ear. 'Go get 'em, girl.'

She rolled her eyes and curved her mouth into a gorgeous smile. 'Fat chance when you're talking about the exciting stuff.'

'I was the entrée, you're the main course.' She'd blow their socks off.

And she did. Tori had every person in that auditorium leaning forwards, ears straining, eyes wide, some mouths open, as they took in the Heart Lady's words, her passion, her need for them to understand hers was grassroots cardiology and that it was as important as every other specialty out there.

During the first video clip of the lad, Thomas, a pin drop would've been loud. He'd always expected the best from her, and she'd delivered, but not to him. She was going from strength to strength, never standing still. Pride swelled inside Ben, filling his lungs and making breathing an effort, warming him throughout and curling his toes. Tori was awesome. Beyond awesome. Her passion for her work poured out of her.

She used to have that depth of passion for me. Or so I thought.

Had Tori plugged into her work when they'd split up? Did this clinic of hers take up all her passion now? Was there any left over for anyone else? Him? The pride remained, but the warmth cooled as reality hit home. Whether she cared for him or not, Tori would never give up her work and, what's more, he'd never ask her to. Tori had found her niche and it was too important to her to ask if she'd consider anything else. *Like there were grounds for her doing so anyway. We haven't returned to that state of bliss where our love conquers all. Yeah, like that worked last time.*

And now, knowing what he did, it sure as hell wouldn't work at all. Ben glanced around, saw the wrap-up clip of Thomas coaching the school team and Tori's audience rising to their feet, clapping hard. *Concentrate.*

'One final thing.' Tori held up her hand for silence. 'Please, please, don't forget the small things in medicine. They're what grow into huge, and often detrimental, problems for our patients. Rheumatic fever is a prime example. Thank you, ladies and gentlemen.'

Luc hugged her before turning to his students. 'The Heart Lady reminds us all why we practise medicine. Never forget this lesson.'

Ben doubted anyone here was ever likely to. Tori packed a mighty punch.

As he knew all too well. What was he going to do about that? They had three days left to explore Paris together. And three nights. Forget the nights. They were banned from being used the way he'd like to. His hand slapped his thigh. Why, when he felt used and deceived, did he still entertain ideas of making love with Tori? Why, when he couldn't drop the whole pregnancy secret, did he want her so badly? What he wanted was to walk away from her at the end of their time in Paris with no lasting hankerings for her, no persistent niggles that he belonged with her, no matter what had gone down between them.

He just had to put more effort into focusing on what was important. Like his father had always told him, 'Whatever you choose to do, be the best at it. Never take second place.' To get that partnership he needed he had to remain focused on the clinic and his work there, not on what might've been or could be with Tori if they hadn't both stuffed it up. Yes, his father might be overbearing and demanding but he did have a valid point.

'You coming?' Tori nudged him none too gently.

Ben glanced around, saw that the crowd of students had dissipated while he'd been miles away. 'Lead on.'

Luc gave them a guided tour of the cardiac unit in his hospital. An entourage followed them all the time, hovering over every word either of them spoke to patients, nurses, doctors, some asking for interpretations.

As they stepped out of one room Tori leaned close to him and whispered, 'This is embarrassing.'

As he inhaled her scent he whispered back, 'The price of fame,' and got a wonky grin in reply.

Luc approached a bed in which a girl lay staring out the window, a book open beside her. 'Letitia, I'd like you to meet the Heart Lady.' Turning to them both, he filled in some details. 'Letitia had a heart attack two weeks ago, cause unknown.'

Ben shut down a gasp. Gasping in front of a patient was a no-no. But a heart attack? She was a child. 'Any history of disease that could've caused heart damage in her early childhood?'

Shaking his head, Luc explained, 'She'd been the picture of health, if her family doctor's notes are anything to go by. It's a mystery. Letitia is fifteen, far too young to be dealing with something like this. Would you read through her notes?' he asked Ben.

'You'll have to interpret.' The girl obviously didn't understand English or he doubted Luc would be discussing her case quite so openly. As he listened to details and test results Tori moved closer to the bed.

'Can I sit down?' she asked Letitia in French.

At least, that was what Ben thought she'd said, because when Letitia nodded, saying, *'Oui,'* Tori sat on the edge of the bed.

Tori talked slowly to the girl, trying to make herself understood. They both laughed over something she'd said. Letitia seemed taken with Tori, talking rapidly, only to stop when Tori held up a hand and grinned at her.

Letitia started again, slower this time, and Tori seemed to be getting the gist of what she was saying, occasionally asking for something to be repeated.

Tori's face had lit up with pleasure. From talking in another language? Or was it Letitia herself that had her reacting like that? Then Tori glanced across the next bed, where a much younger girl lay sleeping. Her eyes widened and that look of love included that child.

Children. That's what flicked the switch to glowing in Tori's eyes. Children. Did Tori remember how they'd talked about having a family once they'd finally established their careers? She'd have been a fantastic mother. So sad that Tori hadn't remarried and had a family with someone else. But he couldn't find it within himself to deny he'd have been envious if she had.

Ben shoved that aside, concentrated on what Luc was saying about Letitia's heart attack. Nothing stood out, apart from the fact she'd gone into arrest while participating in a cycle race. Most bewildering, and downright frightening for the patient and her family. 'No family history of cardiac problems, then?'

Luc shook his head. 'Not that anyone's saying.' Out of earshot of Letitia, he added, 'The mother is a little circumspect about that, which has me wondering if there's a paternity issue. Unfortunately, I don't think I'm ever going to get any further with that line of enquiry.'

Ben nodded. 'It's tricky.'

'Very.'

When they were finally finished on the ward Luc took them down to his office for a much-needed coffee. While he was arranging their order with his secretary, Tori turned to Ben. 'Medicine's the same in every country, every language, isn't it? Those children are so special, fighting hard to overcome their illnesses.'

His mouth got away with him. 'When we were being serious we talked of having two.' Not six.

The colour drained from Tori's face so fast he thought she was about to collapse. Reaching for her, Ben held her arms and gazed into her distressed face. 'Tori, I'm sorry. There's a little gremlin in my head this morning, making mischief.'

'P-put it down, then, w-will you?' she stammered, and pulled away.

'I'll try but I also think it best if we're being completely honest with each other and that means sometimes talking about taboo subjects.'

'Then I'm going to avoid all conversation with you.'

He quirked one eyebrow at her. 'You can do that?' It wouldn't do them any good at all, only bring back the tension between them.

Her shoulders lifted, fell. 'It's that or I avoid you completely, not a very grown-up way to behave, I'd have thought. But possibly necessary.'

Unfortunately he really did want to have some time with her in the hope he could put his failed marriage and his ex-wife behind him. Who knew? If he did it right he might even be able to find a new life with another woman. His gut clenched. No? Okay, maybe not.

CHAPTER TEN

TORI LEANED CLOSE to Ben as the curtain fell for the last time. 'I want to see this show every night I'm here.'

'It's great, isn't it?'

'Amazing, but what have I missed? It was impossible to take it all in.' The colours, music, the beautiful dancing girls and the incredible acts of strength shown by the men—all mesmerising. The Moulin Rouge had lived up to its reputation and then some.

'Let's go,' Ben said.

'What's the hurry?' This had been another one of the most amazing nights of her life. A superb dinner and then the show. She so wasn't ready to call it quits and head back to the hotel and that big lonely bed.

'Taxis will be at a premium. There are hundreds of people needing to get back to their hotels.' He sounded so reasonable. Or was that bored?

'Let's find a bar. No, a nightclub's a better idea. The night's still young.' She couldn't remember the last time she'd been up at one-thirty in the morning for pleasure. Pathetic, really. 'Coming?'

Ben stood up slowly. Reluctantly? 'Sure.'

Tori wanted to shake him. 'Sound a little more enthused, will you?'

'Sure.' He managed a smile that sent heat fizzing

along her veins. That heat never faded, always reminding her how good they'd been together. How good they
could be again.

Tori began pushing her way through the crowd, too
impatient to be polite and stand back for everyone else
to go first. She wanted to get out of there and head for
a club and fun with Ben.

The nightclubs were jam-packed with people spilling out onto the streets, but that didn't deter Tori. At the
third one she grabbed Ben's hand and hauled him inside to the bar. With drinks in hand they squeezed into
a corner and people-watched. Loud music had her blood
pumping and her toes tapping and before she'd had two
mouthfuls of her sparkling water she was up and dragging Ben onto the dance floor.

Not once did Ben pull back or refuse to go with her
as they danced or drank at her whim. He bought her
more water and himself wine, he talked, and when she
wanted to he stood on the dance floor, gyrating his hips
and smiling as she leapt and twirled and shimmied.

'Not that I call this dancing,' Tori gasped once. 'More
like aerobics in a dog kennel.' She was squashed up
against Ben, breast to chest, hips to hips, her body moving against his in time to the music.

Ben smiled in an enigmatic way and continued moving with her. His arms were on her waist, his fingers
splayed so that she felt each and every one of them.
Like he used to do.

I wish I knew what he's thinking. It felt like he cared
for her if he was reverting to his old, loving ways. And
on the night of her life it was getting to be romantic.

Nearly two hours later they arrived back at their hotel
suite. Soft light from the lamps glowed in the otherwise

darkened room. Obviously the maid had been to turn down their beds.

Bed. Tori smiled as she finally got rid of her shoes. She wasn't tired. She should be, but she couldn't find a tired cell in her body. Not a one. Spinning around on her aching toes, she reached for Ben, caught his tie and tugged him close. Very close. Her lips brushed across his. It wasn't enough. She pressed her mouth against his, felt his heat.

Then he pulled away.

'Tori, are you sure you know what you're doing?'

Yes. She was seizing the moment. She wasn't thinking because thinking clogged the brain. She had wanted Ben for days now and no matter what the consequences this was her moment. She already knew her heart was screwed so she had nothing else to lose and everything to gain by trying to find her way back to them. Who knew? Ben might be waiting for the nod from her. 'Yes, Ben, I do.'

Ben held her gaze for a long, tense moment. A moment when the air became charged with anticipation and need and heat. Then he lifted her into his arms and strode through to her room.

As he laid her on the bed she caught his tie again and tugged him down on top of her. She couldn't wait to feel his weight over her body, to have his hard muscles against her softer ones, his length inside her.

When Ben kissed her he wasn't gentle. Instead, his mouth claimed her lips, his tongue thrust into her mouth to dance with hers. Oh, the taste of him. Her Benji. His hands cupped her face, holding her head still, like he'd always done. His elbows kept his weight off her, weight she craved so she knocked his arms sideways to bring him tumbling onto her body. That's when she felt right.

Benji's body covering her, his scent, his heat—it drove her crazy with need.

His kiss was full of urgency. Every thrust of Ben's tongue had Tori crying out with need. Her fingers slid down his back, around his waist, between their pulsing bodies and down over the hard set of his manhood. She was melting. Wet and ready. 'Benji, now. Don't wait. I want you.' How had she gone without him for so long?

Then he left her, his mouth withdrawing, his hands pulling away, the weight lifting from her. 'Benji,' she cried.

'Ben. Call me Ben,' he growled.

Shock mixed with understanding stilled her briefly. So this wasn't about who they were but who they'd become. A chill touched her hot skin then disappeared. Okay, so that was a warning not to expect anything from this, but her body was still waiting feverishly for him. 'Ben, don't keep me waiting.'

His shirt flew across the room. His trousers followed. Then he was back, reclaiming her mouth, his body pressing hers into the mattress. His erection was heavy evidence of how much he wanted this, if nothing else.

Then she was being lifted and the zip at the back of her dress was being tugged down. She stood to shuck out of the silk and stood before him in her lacy black bra and thong, and suspenders with black stockings. She'd gone all out, hoping when she shouldn't have that they'd end up here sometime tonight. It had been a long time since she'd worn lingerie as exquisite as this. Seven years, in fact.

'Tori, oh…' Ben's hands were gentle yet demanding as they touched her breasts, her stomach, thighs with a familiar caress that brought back happy memories of stolen moments between shifts, of making out in their massive super-king-sized bed. 'You're so beautiful.' His tongue was raspy on her skin, heightening the already tight, ready-to-spring-apart feelings dominating her mind and soul. 'I remember this. I've never forgotten.'

Now she was confused. Had he insisted on 'Ben' and not 'Benji' to keep in control? Heat shot through her from that tongue, those fingers stroking her in places that had forgotten what making love was all about, places that remembered instantly and came alive too fast. Thinking just became impossible. 'I have to have you. Now, Ben.'

Ben's growl was primal as he slipped on a condom, then pulled her close, skin to skin for the length of their bodies. His hands were on her waist when she lifted her legs up and around his body. Guiding him inside her, she gasped at the feel of his shaft touching her moist core. Lowering farther, she took him in, inch by hot inch until she had him all.

'Hell, Tori, you're killing me.' He lifted her so he was free, then drove back in, hard and fast, again and again.

And far too quickly Tori exploded, shattering into a million pieces as he reclaimed her. How could she have gone so long without this? Without Benji in her life? In her body?

Tori knew the exact moment Ben left her bed. He was stealthy in his actions, slowly rolling over and sitting up, pausing, then standing and crossing the room. She didn't open her eyes, didn't want to see him leaving her. Refused to beg him to return to bed and hold her.

He'd turn her down anyway. It had been when they had made love the second time, lying across the bed and taking longer to explore each other's bodies, that she'd realised that while Ben's lovemaking was intense he wasn't totally with her, not in sync with her thoughts and emotions. Not like Benji used to make love to her.

That's when she understood she'd lost him, if she'd ever had him, and that she'd been wishing for a rainbow these past days. So she'd held on and tried to stamp every touch and kiss and caress firmly onto her brain to take out later and cherish. It had been hard but she'd refused to let her disappointment turn to hurt and then to anger. Instead, she'd lapped up the loving and then lain curled up against him for the last hour of the night.

The bathroom door clicked firmly shut and then the shower ran for a long time. Washing her off his skin?

Pain hit her in the chest, nearly stalling her heart. Rolling onto her back Tori stared at the ceiling, her fists pushing into her thighs as she fought the longing for Ben, the need to climb into the shower with him, to hold him—for ever. But she had her pride. It was stretched very thin, but it was there.

She did not want to see his rejection in those sombre eyes. She'd break down in front of him if she did. That would have to wait until she was alone.

Ben was going. She knew that with absolute certainty. The pain gnawing at her muscles, her stomach and her heart told her that. She'd finally had the guts to tell him about their baby and in doing so she'd lost him. If she'd ever had him. She'd probably been fooling herself to even think there had been a remote possibility of them getting back together. He'd been distant since Nice. Sure, he'd been friendly and prepared to have fun doing things around Paris, but she'd felt his distance. Last night had been special, and she'd worked hard to ignore what had been going on with Ben, to the point she'd fooled herself.

And now she had to face the glaring truth. Getting back with Benji was never going to happen.

The bathroom door opened.

She rolled onto her side, facing away from the door. She couldn't breathe and it seemed an age before she heard Ben again. She thought he'd come into her room but she couldn't be certain. Everything went absolutely quiet for a long time then she heard soft footsteps on the carpet and it sounded as though something had been placed on the bedside table on the other side of the bed.

A whisper she couldn't decipher.

Footsteps going away, leaving her.

The entrance door opening, clicking shut.

The absolute silence of an empty apartment. Empty except for her. A sound she was familiar with. The pain and loneliness she'd known a long time back.

Hot, scalding tears covered her face, drenched the pillow.

Her body began to shake.

A scream tore up her throat. She clamped her mouth shut, swallowed hard. She would not let it out.

Tori cried and cried and cried until there was nothing left inside her. Then, exhausted, she fell into a restless sleep.

When she woke again it was after midday. Why hadn't the cleaning staff woken her when they'd come in? Who cared? She certainly didn't.

Swinging her legs over the edge of the bed, she turned and saw a folded sheet of the thick hotel paper on her bedside table.

Her fingers shook as she picked it up. 'What have you got to say to me, Ben? Thanks, have a great day? Sorry, but we shouldn't have? No, not that, please.'

It would be easier to ignore the note, leave it and take a long, hot shower, before deciding on her next move.

But it would eat at her, and there'd be no peace until she'd read Ben's last message.

Straightening her back, she snapped open the page and read with a thudding heart.

Dear Tori

I'm heading back to London on an early flight. I didn't want to wake you, considering the little sleep you've had. You need your energy for sightseeing.

'Yeah, right. Like I want to do that now.'

Tori, I'm glad I had this time with you. All of it, including last night. But it is time to go. I've learned that we weren't meant to get back together. Even if we wanted to give it another go I can't give up my career when I have yet to prove myself, and I'd never ask you to leave your clinic.

Take care, sweetheart. You've done so well and I'm sure I'll be reading more about the Heart Lady.

Hugs, Ben.

'Thanks for nothing, Ben, Benji, or whoever the hell you are.'

The pain had gone. She felt numb. She could not feel her heart as it splintered into a thousand pieces. She would not laugh at herself for having been foolish enough to think she and Ben might be able to overcome the past.

Screwing up the page, she threw it at the bin and shuffled into the bathroom and stood under the shower for so long her skin resembled a prune when she turned off the water.

Applying her make-up wasn't easy with her face blotchy and swollen but she persevered and eventually looked half-decent. After drinking the strong coffee she'd ordered from room service she headed out, surprised at the 'Don't Disturb' sign hanging on the outside of the door.

'Caring to the last.'

Slipping into the crowds filling Paris, Tori knew that sitting in her hotel suite, feeling sorry for herself, for the next three days was not an option.

This was her dream city and she would see all she could cram in before getting on the big tin bird and flying home. Back to reality.

Ben almost literally felt his heart crack as he boarded his flight at Charles de Gaulle Airport. No matter he'd known he'd be leaving Tori to return to his life in London, he still wasn't prepared. It wasn't as though he felt free again. Nowhere near free. Hopefully that'd come as he settled back into the demands of the clinic.

On board he was deaf to the announcements from the flight crew, blind to the other people around him, only vaguely aware of the plane hurtling along the runway and lifting into the turbulent summer air.

Staring out the window, he saw nothing as the plane flew across the Channel. Nothing except the running film in his brain.

Tori laughing. Tori under him, her face filled with need and ecstasy. Tori. The guilt turning her eyes dark and her mouth tight as she talked about the baby.

She should've told him at the time she'd miscarried. No matter that he hadn't been spilling his guts about what had been going on in his life. That baby had been theirs, not hers. A baby was life-changing. Losing it had made an impact on Tori. That was apparent in her voice, in her eyes, with the gentle touching of the gold bracelet she'd had made in remembrance of their child.

But he was stuck on the fact that Tori hadn't told him. He'd have dropped everything to be at her side. His career could've taken a back seat for a few weeks.

Had they ever been right for each other? He'd believed so, still wanted to believe it, but the facts showed differently.

Had they been in lust rather than love? No, he wouldn't accept that. He still held her in his heart, and knew he always would. But getting back together was a recipe for disaster when they couldn't tell each other the really important things. It seemed that when the chips were down they reverted to being individuals who didn't communicate, who deliberately kept things from each other. He'd expected total transparency from her.

Hypocrite.

Yep.

But hadn't he stood his ground and faced up to his shortcomings despite the old man's fury? Yep. But he hadn't told Tori. He'd been gutless, hadn't trusted her to love him enough. And now he wasn't trusting her again.

'Can you fasten your seatbelt for landing, sir?'

Ben blinked, stared out and down, saw the green fields of England speeding beneath the wing. 'Sure.'

England. The place he called home these days. He waited for the usual buzz of excitement to touch him. It didn't happen.

He needed a distraction. Not one with long, red hair and eyes the colour of emeralds that filled with excitement and sadness and guilt and laughter. Any old everyday distraction would do fine.

He got one. Striding out into the arrivals lounge, he was greeted by Jason, one of the partners he worked for at the cardiology clinic. 'Hey, Jason, what brings you out here?'

Jason shook his hand. 'How was the conference?' Obviously not in a hurry to answer the question.

'Excellent.'

'I hear your ex was in Nice, and that she went to the Paris teaching hospital, too.'

Jason wasn't afraid of treading on toes—he leapt on them. 'Yes, Tori was in both places. Yes, I spent time with her. No, we're not getting back together.'

'How do you feel about that?'

'Jason, shut up, will you?'

The damned man just shrugged. 'The car's outside the main entrance.'

The car, as in the chauffeured Bentley. 'I'm getting the royal treatment.' Not that Jason wasn't averse to offering his friends a lift, but to have swung by Heathrow seemed a bit extreme. 'What's up?'

'We'll talk in the car.'

Ten minutes later Jason told him, 'Maxwell's not returning to work. He's resigning his partnership. Mary has liver cancer and the prognosis isn't good.'

Ben had known Maxwell's wife was ill but this was worse than anything he'd expected. 'Surely Maxwell can take leave for as long as he wants?'

'He doesn't want to. Says he should've resigned before and now it's almost too late.' Jason stared out at the passing scenery.

'I'm very sorry.' Life was precarious. John's cardiac

arrest had told him that. Friends were precious. As was his ex-wife.

'Of course, Maxwell might change his mind later, and if he does we'll work something out, but right now we have to accept his wishes.'

And I thought I had it bad, leaving Tori in Paris. At least she was fit and well and he knew exactly where to find her if he couldn't control the urge to see her and hold her and kiss her again. But he felt raw. Raw and aching and desperately in need of resolution.

Jason cleared his throat. 'The partners, me included, have been discussing where to from here. We're offering you a partnership.'

Yes. I've done it. Yee-ha. It was hard not to punch the air.

Tori would.

A great lump of pride and gratitude clogged his throat. A partnership in Harley Street. Seven years on from disaster and he'd finally paid his dues. He wanted to tell Tori. First. Then John and Rita, and his family, especially his father. Take that, Dad. Honesty did pay.

Gloating isn't attractive.

Gloating was what his father did. Ben gulped. He didn't want to sound like *him*. Hell, was he like his old man? Shock stunned him. He couldn't be. He could be. Hell. Ben nearly choked. No way. But he was just as driven.

'You can take time to think about it,' Jason said with a dollop of disbelief and a hint of sarcasm in his voice.

Ben turned to him, his face split into an easy smile. 'I don't need to.' But again he hesitated.

Are you sure? Is this what you really want? To be permanently in London? Cutting off any chance of getting together with Tori?

Tori and he were over. Had been since the night he'd walked out of their apartment. These past days had been an aberration, a bit of fun with a woman he'd once loved, still loved. There was no future for them.

Jason's offer was real, waiting for him to sign up. 'This is what I've been working for.'

'That's a yes, then?'

Ben put out his hand. 'Definitely a yes.'

'Good. The partners will be pleased. You're expected at dinner tonight. My place.'

Despair nearly swamped his happiness. Why couldn't he just accept this amazing offer and what it entailed? Hell, he *had* accepted it.

Ben leaned back into the corner of the car and took the glass of champagne Jason held out.

'This is just a quiet toast between you and me.' Jason tapped his glass. 'I knew I'd picked a winner when you came for your interview.'

Sipping the champagne, Ben finally grinned. 'Thanks.' Suddenly excitement gripped him, making him want to shout out to everyone they passed. Partner in a renowned cardiac clinic. Amazing. The only glitch was the reason a partnership had become available.

'You haven't hauled out your phone and told anyone about the partnership,' Jason observed with a wry smile. 'I would forgive you in the circumstances.'

'I'll get to it. At the moment I'm celebrating with one of my partners.' Even while wanting to shout this fantastic news from the rooftops, Ben felt unusually reticent.

Growing up, every time he'd achieved something big and rushed to tell his dad, expecting high praise, he'd got a curt nod and been told to do even better. It had always taken the gloss off his achievement. He didn't want that this time, even if his father wouldn't be the first person he told.

And who would that be? She would only congratulate you and hang up. Is that what you want?

Of course, it started to rain when Ben was farthest from his apartment. 'Typical,' he growled as he ducked into a pub close to Southwark Bridge. But the weather did suit his despondent mood.

'I'll have a pint, thanks, pal,' he told the barman as he settled onto a stool. Looking around at the noisy patrons, he shook his head. What a difference seven days made. This time last week he'd been in a restaurant in Paris, having a wonderful meal with Tori before going to the show. Now John and Rita were ensconced in his apartment with their kids, Tori was back in Auckland, and he'd been made a partner in the Harley Street practice, thereby achieving his goal.

'Here you go.' The barman pushed his drink into his line of vision and waited to be paid.

'Cheers.' Shoving his wallet back into his pocket, Ben took a thoughtful mouthful of the beer, which turned his mouth sour. Nothing wrong with the beer, just his mood. He should be on top of the world.

He missed Tori. That was all. Nothing else bothered him. Much. Tori was everything. Even London wasn't the same without her to talk to, and she had never been here. He hadn't phoned to tell her about the partnership. How could he when he'd left her that note in Paris?

Yeah, moron. Saying you'd learned the two of you weren't meant to get back together wasn't exactly your brightest move.

Gulp. The beer was not getting any better.

Even with his friends here in his apartment, he was

lonely—for Tori. This was worse than when they'd split up in the first place. Then there'd been so much going down he'd had plenty to focus on. Now he had a partnership to sign up for and yet all he wanted was to see Tori, talk about random things, go for a walk with her in those ridiculously high shoes she adored.

'Something wrong with your beer?' the barman asked.

'No.' Ben shook his head. 'Can you get me a vodka, please?'

Tori used to drink the occasional vodka and lime. Towards the end of their relationship she'd been drinking more than the occasional one. He'd known she'd been drowning her sorrows but had never reached out to her because he'd felt too guilty about being the cause of her sadness. He hadn't been able to bear to think that she blamed her drinking for the miscarriage, especially as she hadn't even realised she'd been pregnant. If anyone was responsible, it was him. For pushing her away, instead of leaning on her and telling her how much he needed her.

Tori, Tori, Tori. Always in his head.

Why didn't he just phone her? Now? Say hi, and ask how she was settling back into work after her trip.

Suddenly Ben's phone was in his hand and he was scrolling through his contact list. Tori's number glinted at him, tormenting him to press the phone icon so he could hear her voice, listen to her talk about her young patients and the clinic.

His heart slowed. Should he? What would Tori say when she heard his voice? *Go away and leave me alone*, most likely.

The vodka tasted better. His thumb slid back and forth over the phone. It would be so easy to press the screen and wait for her to pick up. Bang. The phone lay on the counter. Get real. If he phoned and talked to Tori, told her about the partnership, chatted about Nice, then what? Tell her how much he missed her? That would go down like a lead balloon. She'd laugh at him and hang up.

Gulp. The vodka disappeared in record time—for him anyway. He stared at the phone, even though the back light had gone off. When had he got to be such a coward?

'Want another?' The barman was back.

Yep, followed by yet another. 'No, thanks, pal.' Getting drunk only delayed things, didn't solve them. Picking up the phone, he felt a thrill as a text came through. Tori?

Of course not. He pressed the phone icon on the number. 'Hey, Rita, I'll be there in twenty. Want me to bring anything home for dinner?'

'Just that ugly butt of yours. John could do with some company. Apparently the kids and I have driven him crazy.' Rita didn't sound at all perturbed, more like happy.

'He's getting restless, thinks he's ready to be up and at everything, when he's still not a hundred percent well yet.'

'You got it. Are you still at work?'

Not a silly question. It was barely eight. 'I'm in a pub. Got rained on when I went for a walk.'

'Ah, doing the Tori thing. See you soon.'

Ben smiled for the first time all day. Rita got how he missed Tori and didn't take a back seat when it came to mentioning it. Was he missing something here? Apart from Tori? Would this be easy to sort if he actually tried, instead of avoiding it for fear of losing his chance?

CHAPTER ELEVEN

TORI STRAIGHTENED HER aching back and wrote down Dean's latest obs. Had she really been in France last month? Since arriving home three weeks ago she'd barely come up for air. Flu had struck, taking out the staff one by one. This past week Conrad and three nurses had been away.

Operations had been postponed but Tori had refused to cancel any appointments, which meant the waiting room was chock full of families with ill children desperate to see her. Fingers crossed, they were through the worst of it all and would soon be back to full strength.

'At least this young man will be improving very soon.' Dean had become gravely ill and early that morning he'd had surgery for a bleeding stomach ulcer. He'd been brought back to the ward an hour ago, Tori and the gastro surgeon having agreed it was best for Dean to remain under her care rather than add to his distress by moving him to another ward that was full of adult patients.

'He's had more than his share of bad luck,' Karen, the nurse assigned to him, commented.

Dean lay so still Tori wanted to touch him to make sure he was breathing. She knew he was, she'd just done the obs, but his little chest barely rose on every intake of air. It was very tempting to pull up the chair and sit with him for a while, to give him her undivided attention, even when he had his own nurse right there. Anyway, if she sat she'd probably nod off, given the exhaustion dragging at every muscle in her body.

Gently brushing an errant curl off Dean's brow, she told him even though he couldn't hear her, 'That T-shirt will look cool on you.'

'How many did you bring back?' Karen grinned.

'Quite a load. There's a case full of them in my office. Help yourself to one.' Her eyes were still fixed on Dean, her heart crunching for this brave wee man. After a long moment she turned to Dean's parents, sitting apart on the far side of the bed. 'Hey, you two, he's doing well.'

'He's so sick.' Julene began to cry. 'I don't think he's going to make it this time, Tori.'

'Don't say things like that,' Leo snapped, moving his chair farther sideways.

'Look at him. Think what he's been like this past month. He'd even stopped smiling.' The tension between the two of them was at breaking point.

Tori sighed. It was incredibly difficult for them, watching their son fight for his life and not being able to do anything. 'Because Dean's so anaemic it's going to take time before he's completely back to his normal cheery self. Anaemia drains a person of all their energy. He's being given whole blood right now and when he wakes up you'll notice a change in his disposition.'

'Why did he get an ulcer in the first place?' Leo snapped. 'Ulcers are what adults get, not kids.'

'From the information I received about all drugs Dean's been given over the last two years, I suspect those tablets for headaches he took earlier this year may have been the culprit. They're known to cause stomach problems, including ulcers, especially in children.' Why the GP had prescribed them to a child when there was a liquid version available Tori had no idea, but it made her want to scream with frustration. 'That's why pharmacists advise taking those pills with food.'

'I've always made certain he eats before taking anything,' Julene ground out through clenched teeth. 'Always.'

'The good news is that we can safely say the assist device wasn't the cause of Dean's exhaustion. His heart's working just fine.' That had been a load off her mind.

'I guess we can be thankful for that.' Leo crossed his legs, uncrossed them again. 'I can't help wondering what's next.'

'How about a full recovery?' Tori certainly hoped so, and in reality there was no reason why Dean wouldn't be up and about soon. But these two were going to take longer to relax. 'Go take a break. You both need it. Dean's under one-on-one care for the next twenty-four hours so he won't be alone at all. His surgeon will be keeping an eye on him. Go home, have a meal together, get some sleep.' *Make love and remember why you're together.*

She wouldn't have thought that until Nice and Ben. Benji. Pain stabbed her. She missed him so much. Unbelievable considering how long they'd been separated. It had been a mistake to spend time with him, and yet nothing could've stopped her. She loved him, and that had made her careless with her heart.

'I'd feel guilty, going home,' Leo muttered.

Guilt. There was a lot of that about. 'Don't.' Like she had any right to tell him that. 'You're no good to Dean if you're asleep on your feet.' Tori paused, added quietly, 'If you're both arguing because of that tiredness, he's going to pick up on your tension. Do yourselves a favour and get out of here for a while. I'll phone if anything changes but Dean will probably sleep most of the day.'

'Tori.' Julene lifted her head and stared at her. Her tone softened. 'Thank you for everything. Not just the medical stuff but things like this. You understand us and that's been so important all the way through.'

'Get out of here,' she growled, as warmth expanded in her chest. This was why she worked the hours she did, trying to make a difference for a few families. That in turn filled her life with happiness. But it would be so much better if she had Ben with her. Or she was with him. Like that'd ever happen. Watching the couple leave, Leo's arm at last around Julene's shoulders, Tori couldn't help wondering what her own future held in the couple stakes. Right this moment it looked bleak. Ben's face flitted into her mind, making her ache with love. What she wouldn't give to have him here, to be able to lean against him and feel his arms around her, giving her strength.

Since when had she relied on someone else to support her?

Shaking that useless question away, Tori told Karen, 'Call me if anything changes.' But she didn't move.

'Will do,' Karen answered quietly, as she re-tucked the blanket around Dean.

Her next patient was thirteen-year-old Katherine, who'd been born with a congenital heart defect. Tori dug into her case to find a T-shirt in the right size. 'Hey, try this on when you get home.'

Katherine's eyes widened. 'Did you get that for me? Great. Thanks, Tori.' No one called her 'Doctor' around here. It was Tori or the Heart Lady. Patients of Katherine's age and older thought it cool to use her first name.

'Right, so how have you been?'

'Just crackerjack. I'm training for the disabled national bowling team.'

'Go, you.' This girl had already learned that the only way forwards was to keep pushing herself.

The morning wore on, then it was afternoon and the number of patients waiting for Tori didn't appear to have dwindled at all. 'Where do they all come from?' she asked her secretary, who delivered coffee and a sandwich to eat before Tori raced along to see Dean.

Dean had woken minutes earlier, and she wanted to be there to reassure him she was around the place. 'Hey, sleepyhead, you're looking good,' she told him.

'I'm sore. My stomach and head hurt.'

Tori read the charts Karen handed her. Everything looked good. 'You've had an operation, that's why you're uncomfortable. You'll feel better next time you wake up.'

'Not tired.' He was already nodding off, trying to fight sleep but rapidly losing the battle.

'Of course you'd say that. Being tired means being ill to you,' she said in a whisper, as she brushed that same errant curl aside. 'Next time I drop by you'll be asking if you can get up.' Fingers crossed.

'His mum and dad texted to say they'd be back shortly,' Karen said.

She had no excuse to stay with him. Tori sighed. She felt drawn, wanted to watch over him until he was up and laughing and ready to take on the world again. She always felt this way with her patients, as though she could give them some of her energy and strength. Except she didn't have any spare at the moment. 'Guess I'd better go back to my other patients.'

'I hear they're pouring in the doors today.'

'They have been since I got back.' Tori smiled tiredly at Karen, then noticed the nurse's focus was on something behind her. 'What?' She turned, and gasped at the man standing in the doorway. 'Ben?' So her exhaustion had finally caught up with her, had her hallucinating. She'd had a momentary hiccup earlier, craving him, wanting his shoulder to lean on, his arms around her. Seemed she'd wished too hard. Shaking her head, she dashed a hand over her eyes. 'I'm losing my grip on things.' But when she focused on the man again she saw only Benji.

'Tori, sweetheart, it's me.' Those arms she'd wished for were engulfing her, pulling her close to that broad chest she needed to lay her head against. 'I'm real.'

Pine and citrus scent teased her, convincing her sluggish brain. Tipping her head back, she gazed into the most wonderful pair of caramel eyes she'd ever seen. 'Yes, I think you might be.'

Right then she heard Julene say, 'Oh, sorry, are we interrupting something?'

Tori turned in Ben's arms to see Dean's parents hovering anxiously near the door. 'Hey, of course you're not. This is Dr Ben Wells. He's a cardiologist from London.' Though what he was doing here in her clinic she had no idea. 'Ben, I talked to you about Dean. Julene and Leo are his parents.'

As Ben shook their hands he glanced at Dean. 'You replaced the device?'

'No.' As Tori explained Dean's situation she couldn't stop the questions rocketing through her brain. Why was Ben here? Was this a fleeting visit? Had someone in his family taken ill? What was going on?

'Tori?' Karen nudged her. 'Are you all right?'

No. She didn't have time for this. 'I'm fine. Ben, sorry, but I've got a very full schedule for the rest of the day.'

Ben stepped up beside her. 'I heard about your staff shortage due to flu. Need a hand dealing with all those patients lined up in the waiting room?'

I'd love it. Spinning around, she started walking towards her office. 'Are you up to it? When did you land? Had any sleep?'

'I don't think I'm as tired as you appear to be.' He reached a hand to her cheek, ran a finger down to her mouth. 'I got in at seven this morning, have had a few hours' sleep. Anyway, I got bumped up to first class so I slept most of the way over.'

'Then you're on. I feel like I'm taking two steps forwards and three back at the moment.' *And now Ben's here and I still don't know why.*

Ben's hand on her elbow was familiar and worrying. 'Let's get it sorted, then we'll talk.'

Talk? Now, there was a novel idea. 'Thank you for stepping up. I really could do with an extra hand at the moment. In fact, if you didn't already have one on the other side of the world I'd offer you a job right now. The clinic's growing by the week and I need to take on another specialist.' Ben would be the obvious choice—if only he was available.

Ben pulled her to a stop and turned her to lay his hands on her shoulders. 'I've missed you, Tori. More than ever.' His lips brushed hers, returned for a more serious kiss, one that lightened every aching muscle in her body and gave her hope. Hope was dangerous, and probably about to explode in her face. But that was definitely hope flaring in her stomach, her head—her heart.

Tori went looking for Ben, found him in deep conversation with Conrad at Dean's bedside. 'Hey, you two seem to be getting on fine.'

'Why wouldn't we?' Ben asked.

'No reason.' She dredged up a smile for him, automatically reaching for Dean's notes. Glancing down the page, she said, 'All good. Dean, you feeling better now?'

'Yes, Tori. Ben talked to me when I woke up. Have you heard how Maelee's doing?'

'Her doctor in Paris emailed me the other day,' Tori said with a smile. 'He said she's recovering well.'

Glancing at Ben, Tori found his gaze fixed on her. It was time to find out why he'd turned up. If only she didn't feel so lethargic. 'Feel like heading out of here for a bit, going to the apartment maybe? Conrad's feeling well enough to cover the evening rounds and be on call for the night. Which means I can get some sleep.' *After we've talked.* Or would that be better left until after sleep? Falling asleep mid-conversation wouldn't earn her any goodwill.

Ben smiled. 'Sounds like a good idea as long as I can drive. You're beyond it.'

She dug the keys out of the handbag slung across her shoulder. 'All yours.' This being looked out for was a novelty. And she could ask questions on the way home and still get her sleep once she got there.

Some plan that turned out to be. She woke as Ben opened her door of the car at her apartment. 'Come on, sleepyhead.'

'We're home already?' She struggled to stand up, and Ben placed an arm around her waist.

'Home, and I've ordered pizza. It'll be here shortly.'

'I'm not hungry.' Just in need of fifty winks.

'You can't do the hours you've done on one sandwich.' When her eyebrows rose, he nodded. 'Yes, I know what you've eaten today. Next to nothing.'

Ben was in their home for the first time since that

awful day he'd left her. Sure, it was her place now but this was where they'd lived after they'd married, the home they'd picked together. She shivered with trepidation. Why was he here? She couldn't take another knock-back.

In the lounge her eyes locked on the photo she'd framed of them, taken at the Moulin Rouge. About the only thing she had managed to unpack yet. The urn was due to arrive next week.

Ben picked the photo up. 'You looked stunning that night. More stunning than usual,' he added with a smile that reminded her of everything they'd done after the show.

The bell rang, announcing someone in the foyer downstairs.

'That'll be dinner.' Ben headed for the button to open the door.

'Talk about a quick save.' She smiled around a yawn and sank onto the nearest chair.

Barely managing to eat two slices of pizza, Tori found herself yawning again and again. So much for having a meaningful conversation.

'Go take a shower.' Ben nudged her in the direction of her bedroom before she could voice the questions battering her brain.

She managed to mutter, 'When did you get so bossy?' as she staggered through the bedroom to the bathroom. Benji was home. What did that mean?

She'd never felt this tired, not even in the days she'd worked as a registrar. She dozed off, standing upright with a shoulder against the shower wall.

'Hey, come on, Tori. Time you were tucked up in bed.' A hand shook her shoulder gently. 'Benji?'

'Who else would you let into the bathroom with you?' He grinned.

'I am so zonked.'

'I know. It's almost insulting.' He flicked the water off and held a towel out, ready to dry her off.

As she stepped onto the mat she asked, 'How long are you here for?' She could get used to this all too easily.

'I'm home for good.' Ben dried her with the fluffiest towel she owned.

'That's great.' What did that mean? Home, as in where?

'I'm not returning to London, Tori.'

'What about your job?' *Concentrate. Benji's telling me something important.*

'You offered me one today, remember?'

'Don't play games with me, please. I would love you to work with me. I meant that offer. But you work in London.'

He swung her up into his arms and strode through to the bedroom to place her ever so gently on the bed. 'I've given notice. I was offered a partnership and I've turned it down.'

That woke her up. Jerking upright, she stared at him. 'But you've worked hard for that partnership, wanted it more than anything.'

'Have you ever striven so hard for something that you've lost sight of everything else that's important?' Blazing eyes fixed on her.

'Yes.' The clinic. But that had been the intention. The clinic had been her drug of choice to blot out her other dreams—the failed ones all to do with Ben and having a family with him.

Then the tiredness was back, dragging her under even as she fought to stay fully alert.

When Tori woke she couldn't move for the arm

draped over her waist and the warm body pushed hard against her back. 'Ben?'

Then she felt the aches throbbing in every muscle in her body, the pounding in her head. 'I shouldn't have laughed yesterday about not catching the flu.'

'I'll get you some water and drugs,' murmured the only voice she wanted to hear right now.

Ben was back in no time, helping her to sit up, handing her tablets and a glass. 'Now go back to sleep.'

Bossy. But the next thing she knew was waking up again, and Ben was bringing her a warm cloth to wipe her face before presenting her with toast and honey.

'You have to eat.'

'I have to get up. I've got patients to see.'

'All sorted. I'm going in shortly to help Conrad with the appointment list. You'll be all right here?'

Her eyelids were drooping already. 'I'm coming with you,' she muttered, as she slid down beneath the duvet and snuggled into the pillow.

Everything was a blur, days and nights rolling into each other. The only thing Tori knew for certain was that Ben was there a lot, bringing her meals, helping her shower, kissing her cheek, holding her in bed at night. Ben. Her heart. Her love. He'd come back, but why? Something about giving up a partnership. She needed to get to the bottom of that.

Finally she woke with a clear head and no aches anywhere in her body. It had been three days since she'd first crashed. Staggering out of bed, she headed for a shower before getting dressed in something more scintillating than pyjamas.

When Ben got home from the clinic that night he was greeted with the mouth-watering smell of lasagne and the wonderful, heart-stopping sight of Tori looking a hundred percent better than she had since he'd arrived. 'Hey, you're looking almost normal again.'

'I feel better.' There was hesitancy in those green eyes as she handed him a glass of wine. 'Thanks for taking care of me and the clinic.'

'No problem. I enjoyed it. Even looking after the world's grumpiest patient.' Ben placed the glass on the bench before engulfing her in a big hug, quickly following up with a kiss. A proper, lips-on-lips kiss now that the flu had gone. She tasted sweet and exciting, and it would take very little to ignite the flare of desire burning in his groin. But he wasn't following through until they'd talked.

Tori pulled away. 'Why did you leave me that note in Paris? Why didn't you say goodbye properly? That hurt, Ben.' If the past had taught her anything, it was to be honest about how she felt.

Ben winced, hating the thought he'd upset her. 'I was scared, Tori. We'd bared our souls to each other in Paris, but I was too busy dwelling on the past to believe we had a future. I made a mistake.'

'So what's changed? Why did you turn that partnership down?'

'Because I came to my senses. When the excitement didn't kick in after I was offered it I did some soul-searching and it finally dawned on me that, yes, I had been hurt about the baby, but to throw away another chance with you because of that would be right up there with the worst things I've ever done.'

Tori's eyes widened but she didn't say a word. Was that good or bad? He felt a band tighten around his gut. What if she didn't want to give him another chance?

He laid his heart on the line. All or nothing was the

way to go. Then if she kicked him out he couldn't say he hadn't tried hard enough. 'I love you more than anything in the world so why wasn't I here with you? That's what I asked myself.' Not a peep came out of those tempting lips. He continued, 'I do love you, Tori. So much that I want to start over, with you, with my career, with a family if you still want one, with a home I can share with you. This time, I'll keep my priorities straight.'

Now shut up. He did, but his gut was roiling and sweat trickled down between his shoulderblades. Everything rode on what Tori said next.

Tori folded her arms across her chest and eyeballed him. 'You're absolutely certain about that?'

'Tori.' His mouth dried up. Taking a chance, he cupped her beloved face between his hands. 'I'm here for you. Because of you. I can't stay away any longer. Those days in Nice and Paris showed me the truth of my heart. I love you. I have never stopped loving you.'

'Benji.' Tears spilled down her face, over his hands. 'I tried to get over you, thought I'd succeeded, only to learn I'd been telling myself a load of porkies all the time. I'm done with hiding my feelings. When I gave you my heart on our wedding day it was for ever, no matter what happened. I've never reclaimed it. It's still yours.'

Relief was sharp and welcome. He had to kiss her again. As his mouth covered hers the woman of his dreams finally leaned in against him and lifted her arms up around his neck.

She pulled her mouth away briefly. 'Welcome home, Benji.'

When she said 'Benji' with so much love he knew they'd be okay. He was so lucky. She'd given him another chance. He swore this time he'd be a lot more careful with her love. It was far too precious to treat any other way. Sure, there would be problems along the way. But this time they'd face them together.

'I love you with everything I've got, Tori.' His lips brushed her forehead, her mouth, down her throat and onto her breast. 'This is me, for real. Let me prove how real.'

Silently she took his hand and led him to her bedroom, where she undressed first him and then herself. On the bed he covered her body with his, then pushed gently inside her. 'That real enough for you?' he whispered by her ear.

'Oh, yes.' She tightened around him, drawing him in deeper so that he filled her completely. 'Oh, yes.'

He hadn't known it was possible to make love so slowly, so intensely and tenderly. His body melted as desire tightened and tightened and sent them both soaring into oblivion.

Six months later...

Ben leaned close to Tori and whispered in her ear something that made her blush scarlet.

She elbowed him lightly in the ribs. 'No one ever gets their wedding present until after the wedding.'

Ben groaned. 'You mean I have to wait until this crowd have listened to our vows, eaten five courses at Porcini's Restaurant and danced half the night away?'

'I'm worth it, I promise.'

'That's my line.' He winked.

Happiness welled up inside her, blocked her throat as she gazed into the eyes of the man she was about to marry for the second time. This time it would be for ever. She knew they'd finally got it right, and that they'd grown, changed and yet were still the same couple with the same kind of loving going on between them.

A very trim-looking John, holding Rita's hand, approached them, with their two girls bouncing along beside them. He asked with a grin, 'So it's to be a small wedding, eh?'

Ben shook his head. 'Tori has no idea what small means. Apart from the usual family and friends, I reckon she's invited all the clinic staff and every patient she's ever treated.'

Tori nudged him again. 'You do exaggerate.' But not by much. She looked around and her smile grew. Everyone important to her was here. With one exception—Ben's father couldn't bring himself to accept her back into the family. His attitude had hurt them both, but Ben had refused to beg, so his mother had come without him. That had to be one of the few times she'd ever stood up to him. Bet Jeffery didn't know about the coffee dates and shopping for baby clothes that his wife and Tori had once a week.

Her hand automatically rubbed a light circle over her slightly swollen stomach. *How you doing in there, little one?*

'Pregnancy is making you glow.' Rita was smiling and crying and reaching for her hand.

Tori's eyes moistened. 'Stop it. I can't cry and wreck my make-up.'

'Why not? It's your wedding.'

'I am so glad you came over for this.' They'd kept in regular contact since Nice.

'You don't think we'd let you get married without us attending? Besides, John is thrilled to be working at your clinic for the next month while you take that honeymoon.'

'You mean while we shift into that massive house

and start redecorating. Nothing like lying on the beach at some exclusive resort.' But exactly what she wanted to be doing.

'You forgot to add that you'll be popping into work during that time.' Rita's gaze settled on her husband. 'I still remind myself every day how lucky we've been.'

'Sometimes we all need a wake-up call.' Again Tori's hand touched her tummy. Getting past week fourteen had been long and worrisome, but they were there now and she refused to worry any more. This baby would be safe and healthy.

Ben draped an arm over her shoulder. 'Why do they take so long to incubate? I want to meet my child now.'

Shaking her head at her impatient almost-husband, Tori laughed. 'There's not much you aren't impatient about.'

'Then let's get cracking.' Ben clapped his hands to get everyone's attention. 'Time to rock, folks. Can you start making your way down to the wharf? Like as quickly as possible? I'm done with waiting to marry this beautiful woman. The sooner we've had the ceremony the sooner we can come back inside the restaurant and begin the reception.'

He leaned close to Tori and added, sotto voce, 'Why *did* you order five courses? Wouldn't one have been enough? Anyone would think you don't want to go to bed with me tonight.'

'Believe me, I want nothing more, but I kind of like making you wait.'

'I've been waiting seven years, woman.' He might have growled, but those caramel eyes were filled with laughter and love. The perfect recipe for a wedding.

To hell with her lipstick. Tori stretched up on her very high heels—bought in Paris, of course—and kissed her man hard, until Rita and John each took an elbow and separated them.

'Come on, you two. There's supposed to be a wedding going on at the marina,' John said. 'We'd hate to miss it.'

'Not a chance.' Tori slipped her hand around Ben's arm. 'Not a chance.'

* * * * *

MILLS & BOON®
Hardback – September 2015

ROMANCE

The Greek Commands His Mistress	Lynne Graham
A Pawn in the Playboy's Game	Cathy Williams
Bound to the Warrior King	Maisey Yates
Her Nine Month Confession	Kim Lawrence
Traded to the Desert Sheikh	Caitlin Crews
A Bride Worth Millions	Chantelle Shaw
Vows of Revenge	Dani Collins
From One Night to Wife	Rachael Thomas
Reunited by a Baby Secret	Michelle Douglas
A Wedding for the Greek Tycoon	Rebecca Winters
Beauty & Her Billionaire Boss	Barbara Wallace
Newborn on Her Doorstep	Ellie Darkins
Falling at the Surgeon's Feet	Lucy Ryder
One Night in New York	Amy Ruttan
Daredevil, Doctor...Husband?	Alison Roberts
The Doctor She'd Never Forget	Annie Claydon
Reunited...in Paris!	Sue MacKay
French Fling to Forever	Karin Baine
Claimed	Tracy Wolff
Maid for a Magnate	Jules Bennett

MILLS & BOON®
Large Print – September 2015

ROMANCE

The Sheikh's Secret Babies	Lynne Graham
The Sins of Sebastian Rey-Defoe	Kim Lawrence
At Her Boss's Pleasure	Cathy Williams
Captive of Kadar	Trish Morey
The Marakaios Marriage	Kate Hewitt
Craving Her Enemy's Touch	Rachael Thomas
The Greek's Pregnant Bride	Michelle Smart
The Pregnancy Secret	Cara Colter
A Bride for the Runaway Groom	Scarlet Wilson
The Wedding Planner and the CEO	Alison Roberts
Bound by a Baby Bump	Ellie Darkins

HISTORICAL

A Lady for Lord Randall	Sarah Mallory
The Husband Season	Mary Nichols
The Rake to Reveal Her	Julia Justiss
A Dance with Danger	Jeannie Lin
Lucy Lane and the Lieutenant	Helen Dickson

MEDICAL

Baby Twins to Bind Them	Carol Marinelli
The Firefighter to Heal Her Heart	Annie O'Neil
Tortured by Her Touch	Dianne Drake
It Happened in Vegas	Amy Ruttan
The Family She Needs	Sue MacKay
A Father for Poppy	Abigail Gordon

MILLS & BOON®
Hardback – October 2015

ROMANCE

Claimed for Makarov's Baby	Sharon Kendrick
An Heir Fit for a King	Abby Green
The Wedding Night Debt	Cathy Williams
Seducing His Enemy's Daughter	Annie West
Reunited for the Billionaire's Legacy	Jennifer Hayward
Hidden in the Sheikh's Harem	Michelle Conder
Resisting the Sicilian Playboy	Amanda Cinelli
The Return of Antonides	Anne McAllister
Soldier, Hero...Husband?	Cara Colter
Falling for Mr December	Kate Hardy
The Baby Who Saved Christmas	Alison Roberts
A Proposal Worth Millions	Sophie Pembroke
The Baby of Their Dreams	Carol Marinelli
Falling for Her Reluctant Sheikh	Amalie Berlin
Hot-Shot Doc, Secret Dad	Lynne Marshall
Father for Her Newborn Baby	Lynne Marshall
His Little Christmas Miracle	Emily Forbes
Safe in the Surgeon's Arms	Molly Evans
Pursued	Tracy Wolff
A Royal Temptation	Charlene Sands

MILLS & BOON®
Large Print – October 2015

ROMANCE

The Bride Fonseca Needs	Abby Green
Sheikh's Forbidden Conquest	Chantelle Shaw
Protecting the Desert Heir	Caitlin Crews
Seduced into the Greek's World	Dani Collins
Tempted by Her Billionaire Boss	Jennifer Hayward
Married for the Prince's Convenience	Maya Blake
The Sicilian's Surprise Wife	Tara Pammi
His Unexpected Baby Bombshell	Soraya Lane
Falling for the Bridesmaid	Sophie Pembroke
A Millionaire for Cinderella	Barbara Wallace
From Paradise...to Pregnant!	Kandy Shepherd

HISTORICAL

A Mistress for Major Bartlett	Annie Burrows
The Chaperon's Seduction	Sarah Mallory
Rake Most Likely to Rebel	Bronwyn Scott
Whispers at Court	Blythe Gifford
Summer of the Viking	Michelle Styles

MEDICAL

Just One Night?	Carol Marinelli
Meant-To-Be Family	Marion Lennox
The Soldier She Could Never Forget	Tina Beckett
The Doctor's Redemption	Susan Carlisle
Wanted: Parents for a Baby!	Laura Iding
His Perfect Bride?	Louisa Heaton

0915 GEN STD LP

MILLS & BOON®

Why shop at millsandboon.co.uk?

Each year, thousands of romance readers find their perfect read at millsandboon.co.uk. That's because we're passionate about bringing you the very best romantic fiction. Here are some of the advantages of shopping at www.millsandboon.co.uk:

* **Get new books first**—you'll be able to buy your favourite books one month before they hit the shops

* **Get exclusive discounts**—you'll also be able to buy our specially created monthly collections, with up to 50% off the RRP

* **Find your favourite authors**—latest news, interviews and new releases for all your favourite authors and series on our website, plus ideas for what to try next

* **Join in**—once you've bought your favourite books, don't forget to register with us to rate, review and join in the discussions

Visit **www.millsandboon.co.uk**
for all this and more today!